THE WIDOW OF FORTUNE

A SINS OF THE FLESH NOVELETTE

ASH RAVEN

Map designed using Inkarnate

Edited by DerpyWickedFox Editorial

Cover art by Rowan Woodcock

No part of this book was created using AI (Artificial Intelligence)

Sometimes, you re-watch *The Gentleman* and get
inspired by Rosalind Pearson

Contents

Within these pages...   VII

Founding and notable members   IX

1. Jackdaw   1

2. Carmela   14

3. Carmela   25

4. Jackdaw   44

5. Carmela   52

6. Carmela   61

7. Jackdaw   79

8. Jackdaw   88

9. Carmela   96

10. Jackdaw   113

11. Carmela   132

Thank you for reading!   142

Also by Ash Raven   143

Within these pages...

Thank you for picking up my soft, dark Monster Romance series, Sins of The Flesh. This is an adult romance featuring a formally exiled Birdfolk and his human love. Please read through the warning below to prepare yourself, and know that this is not an exhaustive list.

CONTENT TAGS:

Plus size female lead, Birdfolk/shifter male lead, Morally grey MCs, Reincarnation, Fated mates, Insta lust (but not love), Vow of celibacy

TRIGGER WARNINGS:

Dubious consent (nonsexual, but nude FMC), blood sharing magic, Suicide (aftermath of a loved one, graphic), Murder (on page), Violence, Blood and gore, Body horror, Domestic violence (emotional and physical (not FMC), mentioned on page, historic), Infertility, Kidnapping, Blackmail, Graphic sex (consensual)

SEX RELATED KINKS:

Power exchange dynamic, Virginity kink, Femdom, Worship, Bondage, Cockwarming, Food play (slight), Being given permission to go feral, Unprotected sex, Praise and degradation, Sex under the influence (marijuana), Sex in semi-public places

If you think a warning was missing here, please send me an email at ash@authorashraven.com

Founding and notable members

Augustine Ravenscroft (he/they)

Deg'Doriel 'Father Doug' (he/him)

Ramón Lagarto (he/him)

Orthia Moore (she/her)

Kragnash 'Nash' Hawthorn (he/him)

Nora Birch (she/her)

Arlo O'Shea (he/it)

WILD WOODLANDS TRUST
HARBOUR CREST
HISTORIC DISTRICT
PASPAWA
RIVER
RIVERFRONT
DOCKLANDS
SOUTH SHORE
GWENMORE
FOUND 1667

Jackdaw

2 Days (1873)

My sobs echo around the room as I pluck the second eye from my love's ashen face. They sound like hers from that night. She was never meant to see my true form. She wasn't meant for that sort of horror. I can't let her vision in the afterlife be tainted this way.

It is better to see nothing than the destruction I have wrought upon her home.

Her body sways slowly like one of the many chandeliers that hang about her grand home. It's all she wanted, grand things. It's why I would fly around Gwenmore's busy districts, plucking jewels and shining baubles from the hats of the high society folk. All to please her. Perhaps this is why she chose the foyer stairwell, dressed in her finest jewels and the special hairpin I gave her.

To shine for all to see when they found her cold body.

I mimicked every sound I could, trying to parse out a sentence to express my deep feelings for her while I remained in my diminutive form. Even though she only knew me as a bird on her balcony and not the cursed creature I truly am, there was care in her eyes when she dropped crumbs on the bannister for me. My devotion to my mate was absolute and I was content to watch her from that distance to keep my love for her safe and secret.

I wasn't able to do either of those things in the end.

Somewhere in the house, there is a soft click of a window unlocking. They have come for me, but I can't leave my sweetness. I nuzzle tighter to her icy cheek and pray to the old gods that we shall meet in the afterlife. We are meant to be together, I can feel the threads of fate that have been cut short by her death.

Their footsteps are dampened by the boogeyman's rolling wave of black sand that carries them down the stairs like aristocrats instead of sneak thieves breaking into my sweetness's manor. Below me stand the three beings who will judge my fate, the monsters who will end my life so I may join my fated on the other side.

Augustine Ravenscroft's finery is as splendid as always, with a top hat resting over blond hair, and his moustache curled perfectly around his lips. He must have been in attendance at The Gin Palace's grand opening this evening. Perhaps in his haste to return, he will unleash his sands on me and pierce my heart first.

Next to him, a much more casually dressed monster stands. He wears a grey sack jacket and matching trousers, but the golden points on his tusks tell me he isn't the working class orc he wants our people to see. Kragnash Hawthorn was high born, and that is a part of himself that can never be stripped away by his clan. At his feet, his war hound stands guard, as undying as he is. The orc turns his head in Augustine's direction and the red jewels encrusted in those tusks catch my eye. Oh, how my love would have shined with those.

I'm most afraid of the demon. He may wear the skin of a priest, but we both know what lies beneath the skin of a man is his true self. Deg'doriel doesn't reveal his giant, purple form often, and I have only been so unfortunate as to see it once. His whiplike tail and crown of horns reveal what a vicious demon lord he actually is.

All of the beings below me sit higher among our monstrous food chain than I, and yet in my final moments of life, I am the one who looks down upon them. It's poetically fitting. They may understand suffering and loss, but they do not know what it's like to see grotesque terror and hatred on your true love's face upon seeing your visage.

My beak will forever carry the facture of her fear of me. The vase she threw at me is still shattered on the blood-stained floor of her bedroom.

"Mr. Torrence," Kragnash calls. "You know why we are here."

"Yes, it's about Tuesday." Broken words, a mix of accents following each syllable, crumble off my beak. I can't mimic the right cadence of speech in my state.

"Jackdaw, you ripped out her husband's insides in front of the family staff, and look what has happened to the woman you claimed to be defending," Ravenscroft states the crimes I committed two days ago as a known fact, but they did not see what he was doing to my sweetness. She would have died then if I hadn't stopped that vile human. "And you have removed her eyes because?"

"To protect her in the afterlife," I bemoan, another sob breaking my speech.

"There's no protection you can offer her soul," Deg'doriel sniffs. "Now get your feathered ass down here."

There isn't much I can do now. My heart is shattered further by his words. The sooner we are done with this pointless judgement, the sooner I shall be with my love again. I touch my forehead to her cheek one final time before I fall from her shoulder. My black wings spread out wide to slow my descent as I transfigure into a more acceptable state for them.

My morning coat flutters around my bent knees as I shake out my body from its disguised form. My clothing shifts with me, a blessing given to me by the old gods. My feathers and wings are stuffed into this black suit, but I prefer it this way, just as I prefer my black riding gloves to hide my talon tipped fingers and my long hooded cloak when I must leave the safety of my nest.

Everything I wear is to hide the monster I am.

On the floor now, my judges stare down at me with intensity. They have all killed humans before. My crime was simply being caught. There are rumours circulating our growing city that an evil haunts this house and will lead to the downfall of all who stay here. The staff describe me as a vile demon, and I suppose they are right now that I have taken a human's life so violently.

How else could a mortal categorise what they saw that night?

"My only request," I say, speech fluttering off into the sound of porcelain shattering. "Is to have my body laid next to hers so we can be together in death."

"We are not going to kill you, Jackdaw," Augustine answers.

"What?" I croak. "No, the rules of our community are clear. You must—"

"Look here, you feathered prick," Deg'doriel lashes out suddenly. He wraps his fist around my throat, his human suit combusting and revealing his purple form. Hellfire burns along his shoulders, his horns, in his eyes. "Our decision is final. You've caused trouble for our way of life, so a price must be paid."

"We've voted on a punishment that we believe fits your crimes, Mr. Torrence." Kragnash steps up and places his hand on the demon's arm. Deg'doriel sets me back on the floor. "For the crime of exposing us to the humans and forming a relationship with one, you're to be banished from the city for one hundred and fifty years, or until you perish, whichever comes first."

No.

Dread drips down my throat like tar until I'm choking with it. This cannot be. Unless taken from me in an act of violence, my life will go on, as unending as the trees out west. Do they not see how sadistic this punishment is? To force this penance upon me is beyond cruelty, for the rest of my days I will suffer this heartbreak alone and unable to truly mourn the loss of my sweetness.

Ravenscroft produces a sealed envelope from his jacket and a flash of gold catches my eye: a small brooch shaped like a bee. What an odd adornment for a man of his stature.

He hands me the letter of dismissal, as if I am simply being removed from work or tenancy.

"Leave by dawn," he states.

"And if we see you again before your time's up, our reunion won't be one of pleasantries," Deg'Doriel growls, before exploding in another burst of hellfire.

They leave me the way they came. I fall to my knees, crumbling their letter in my fist. Though I have survived, my heart has died.

54750 Days

It's pissing rain the day of my return. The October weather is fitting I suppose, as all other aspects of my life have been met with this same dreariness. You kill one human in your long life, so the gods serve you karmic justice for the rest of your days. It's been one hundred and fifty years since I killed one, and still fortune doesn't smile upon me. Flying from treetop to clothes lines to guttering, I make my way from the new expansive west side of Gwenmore towards the area I once knew. Some buildings have changed, and the cobbled streets are paved over, but it's still my old haunt.

I weave through narrow alleys until the world opens upon the great church at the top of the city.

Our Lady of Mercy.

It's out of place amongst the rest of the city. Unlike the buildings that line the street it faces, this monolith is gothic, with limestone flying buttresses and gables that make one think of fifteenth century European churches rather than the Greek revivals that take up main street. It looms over the city with a darkness that fits its inhabitant.

The demon stands before a crowd dressed in black, gathered on the steps of the church as four men carry a decorated coffin inside. If he senses my presence, it doesn't show on his human face. The funeral service will keep him away long enough for me to find what I am looking for.

I swoop around the new fountain and glide through the graveyard. No one has been buried here for a century, the land already overflowing with bones. But the plot I am looking for will not have a dilapidated headstone, nor will it be in one of the great mausoleums near the edge of the consecrated grounds.

My sweet will have been laid to rest beyond this holy place after what happened. Through a thicket of trees, fifty yards or so from the last grave, there is a second cemetery. Contained only by a large circle of stones, this is where the sinners are buried.

Deg'Doriel has been kind to these poor souls, it seems. The grounds are tidy enough, and it looks like more stones have been placed at the head of each. When I look closer, there are two years carved into each, birth and death.

My love will be easier to find then. I hop from each rock, plucking weeds and vines from them until I find a stone with the correct dates. Only then do I transform.

Creaking bones and fluttering feathers are silent against the downpour that batters the tree canopy above. From inside my leather jacket, I pull out the letter Augustine gave me years ago and tuck it under the makeshift gravestone. I have served my penance.

My beak parts and her soft voice comes out of my mouth. It's a melody she would hum while doing her needlework crafts on the balcony. I used to sit and listen to her for hours. Time moved so much slower then that I never thought our days would be cut short. This is the last sound of hers I can mimic. Her voice is lost to time, and the words of praise she would whisper to me as she set down crackers for me to eat are all gone. There is nothing else left but these notes.

In the distance, there is a sob. Muffled by the rain, yet loud enough I know I could make the same noise. I suck in a breath as my body shifts back, shrinking to the forest floor before I venture up into the branches.

A woman stands under the pediment of the last mausoleum. She wears the shroud of a widow, but even from here I can tell she is young by today's standards. A kindred soul then, having lost her lover in her youth.

I can't take my eyes off her form. The severity of her attire fits the occasion, yet she softens it. The curves that can't be hidden under matronly black garb shine through against the worn marble behind her. I must get closer to her and truly see her, even on this dark morning.

Whatever is drawing me to her is mystical, and I have never denied the undercurrent that rules us all. The threads of fate that weave our world together must be followed, or else they snap. Perhaps it is nothing, and I'm doomed to repeat history again. But if the gods have truly forgotten us, perhaps I will find my love again.

Quietly, I make my way to the widow and drop down to the ground just behind her. From here, I can see the supple curves of her calves and the sensibility of her kitten heels. Even sopping wet, she stands straight, her elegance apparent. Rhythmically she squeezes her hand into a fist and I catch glimpses of glitter-painted nails. Forever drawn to these light bending objects, I scurry closer until I'm at her side.

Her sobs have stopped now, but sniffles still echo off the columns. Finally, by the blessings of the gods, she lifts her veil and I see her face.

My heart quakes at the vision before because surely she can't be my lost love. I can't believe what I'm seeing. The gods would not be so cruel, yet here before me she stands.

The sound of shattering porcelain echoes from my mouth, our last moments together flashing through my mind. The woman before me shrieks, and I memorise the sound. Her phone falls out of her hand, bejewelled with fake rhinestones and plastic pearls that call to me. I move quickly to pick it up for her. Careful of my beak, I offer it up to her. She looks at me curiously, and I hold her gaze. Her eyes are dark and her pinned hair is a warm brown colour that I want to bury my beak into.

She is my mate.

I know that for a fact. Every one of my feathers and every beat of my heart begins to weave a metaphysical tapestry of our future together. My sweetness has found me again through time, our frayed threads mending themselves. We must simply join them to start again.

"Jesus Christ, you scared me," she whispers. "Are you giving me my phone back?

A shiver rushes through my body. The voice of a goddess, an angel upon high, speaks to me tenderly. This woman and my sweetness of days past must share one soul, for why else would the gods bring us here?

I step closer and raise her phone to her. She crouches down carefully and then presents her hand to me. Instead of dropping it like she thinks I might, I climb into her warm palm. She makes a little face, probably concerned about what sort of disease a bird might carry, but doesn't bat me away. Another thread of our future is tucked into place.

We are nearly eye level once she raises her hand, and my knees are weak at the sight of her beauty up close. Her round cheeks are dusted with rouge and a deeper red coats her lips. Despite the sobs I heard, not even a fleck of her makeup is out of place. In fact, I wouldn't believe she had been crying at all if I hadn't heard the sounds.

She is an angel, full of grace and glory even surrounded by the macabre. Her dark eyes sparkle as she takes her phone back.

"Thank you, sweetheart."

Oh gods.

I don't know what to say, and my tongue twists into a noose inside my beak. She holds my gaze for a long while, a smile curving on her lips before she lowers her hand back to the marble again. *No, don't make me leave you so soon, my angel.*

"Mrs. Wisniewski," a voice shouts through the storm. "Are you ready to go home, dear?"

She sighs, the smile falling from her lips as she pulls her shroud back over her features. She sets me down and stands up quickly. This person doesn't bring light into her life, yet she is resigned to go when they call. My mate should not be at anyone's whim. They should serve her and only her.

"Stay warm and fly free when the storm has stopped," she says, before stepping into the rain once again.

I watch her join a much older woman, who takes my mate's free arm and tucks her in close under an umbrella. Slowly, they proceed down the cobbled path to a black town car. My body shifts before I can think, so now I can stand tall and see her better.

When she looks back, I know she sees me. Yet she doesn't shriek in surprise. She raises her hand in goodbye, and without thinking, so do I.

But this isn't goodbye.

Chapter Two

Carmela

34 Days

"What were you doing out in the rain, honey?" Dotty asks, as the car turns down one dreary street to the next, Our Lady of Mercy fading into the dark grey morning behind us.

"Just a moment of privacy," I lie, dabbing my face with a napkin to dry the rain and leftover tears.

"Who was that man?" she asks.

"Another widower." I don't know, but when he raised an oddly long gloved hand, I couldn't stop myself from waving back. Through the rain I could see he was wearing some sort of dark jacket that was unnaturally shaped, and his face...

"Have you considered finding a grief support group? I know Our Lady has a few, the Tuesday night one is closed, but I can speak with that Margie woman or Father Doug..."

"It's fine, Dotty, and not what I'm paying you for."

After the reading of Jordan's will and ensuring that I would inherit all of his vast wealth, I hired one Miss Dorothy Lief to be my companion. She's sixty years old and refuses to call me by my first name because it's something I shouldn't give away. It's always "honey," "dear," or worst of all, "Mrs. Wisniewski."

But she is very good at deterring the hangers-on from approaching me. Apparently, many people believed they were going to get a slice of the "Wiz Kid" empire. Jordan was quite the tech genius and businessman. Top investors and former partners assumed their close relationship would have earned some of his wealth. Certainly the long, long line of women who sobbed at his funeral did as well.

But Dotty perfectly commanded every conversation and steered the mourners away from me long enough I was able to slip outside for a breath of fresh air.

In my original master plan, I thought a bodyguard would be my best course of action. Money attracts a dangerous sort of person, the kind that believes they are above the law. Jordan certainly didn't mind *investing* his money in untraceable places. The group of men at the back of church with their barely-concealed guns were enough to prove that.

At her interview though, this slight, grey-haired woman with strange freckles and a carpet bag insisted she was best suited for the role of my bodyguard. After a trial event, the charity auction at the Harbour Crest Yacht Club that was nearly a full disaster, Dotty proved spectacularly fit to prevent people from annoying me.

She was also excellent at clearing the way for our escape after that gas leak explosion or whatever they are claiming blew up the Bradshaw yacht. I certainly wasn't going to speak with police about the odd pair of women hunting him at the party. Whatever that dick did to them, he probably deserved it.

I hired her on the spot permanently and after a month, she has been my best investment since.

We spent the rest of the short car journey from Our Lady to my new residency on the eastern edge of the Historic District in silence. The townhouse is a Greek revival design, built in the mid 1800s but completely renovated on the inside. Jordan purchased this home shortly after we returned from our honeymoon. It was supposed to be our perfect family home, a surprise gift to me once I'd fallen pregnant. Something that we both realised would never happen.

We were never able to conceive the bouncing baby boy he wanted. It's not something I ever wanted, but when money isn't an object I supposed raising a child wouldn't be that difficult, and would make him happy.

I convinced myself that if he was happy, I would be, too. Even at the expense of my own needs.

When it was confirmed by specialist after specialist that I couldn't have children, the sanctity of our marriage fell to shambles. Jordan didn't believe in divorce, but I could see the change in his eyes. Gone was the pride of having a young and pretty wife to parade around parties while he rubbed elbows with every other elitist fuckwad in this city. Now there was only shame.

No matter what I did for him after that, it could never be what he convinced himself that he deserved.

The real surprise gift was finding it amongst the other random assets he owned. I expected some oddities; the portion of a security company, interests in foreign mining operations, properties across the globe. But a grand old house like this one stuck out as an antithesis of my dead husband's investments. When I asked the lawyers about it as well, they claimed Jordan got it for a steal because everyone claimed it was cursed after the first owner committed a brutal murder-suicide there in the 1870's. Everyone who lived here afterwards always moved on quickly.

If you ask me, it's the perfect sort of place to live on your own. Each room is decorated to a different one of my tastes. There isn't a single bit of Jordan in the main part of the house, and I plan to keep it that way for as long as I live. There will never be another man allowed to stay in this house for more than a night—or even for more than the twenty minutes it would take to fuck him.

Never again will I be shackled to a man.

When I married Jordan, I was young and dumb, but at the age of twenty there was nobody to tell me that marrying a man nearly forty years old was a bad idea, especially not when his bank balance had that many zeros. That doesn't even bring into question the assets and investments Jordan had in his portfolio.

They all smiled and took pictures as my father walked me down the aisle. My mother cried happy tears for me at finding a good, catholic man who promised to provide for me and love me forever.

I wonder if she is crying now from her cabana in Mexico? That is where Jordan retired them both after our honeymoon. They were ecstatic at the idea of getting to enjoy the second half of their life somewhere tropical. Not once have they called me since moving a decade ago.

That wasn't the first time Jordan's need to be the only person in my life cropped up, but when I look back at our ten years of marriage, it's the first time that made me think, why would he do this? My family is sixth generation Italian-American. My grandpa used to claim his great aunt's ghost haunts some house in this city. So why would my new husband move my parents so far from Gwenmore?

It happened over and over again. That friend I would go shopping with was a bad influence. My best friend from high school drank too much at dinner and was unsafe to be around. The new girl at the country club was *too* ambitious and I shouldn't be her friend.

I stopped questioning his choices when I thought I would make us happier.

While I could have whatever I wanted, Jordan was always there to make sure my wants were to his taste. I could go wherever I pleased, but on Jordan's time frame. He was an old-fashioned man, the kind that wished for the 'glory days' of the 1950s. When girls were girls, and men were men, as he used to tell me. He needed me at home, or at church, or with dinner in the oven and drink waiting for him.

The driver pulls up to the curb and gets out to open my door. Rain pelts down on her umbrella as she waits for me to climb out. I wonder momentarily if the weather is some sort of sign from the universe, but I have long given up on those. There is no higher power, there is no magic in this world. There are facts, tangible evidence, reality, and that's it. Hearsay and gossip don't hold up in the court of law, so why should it in my life?

"I'd like the rest of the day to myself," I say to Dotty before I get out of the car.

"Are you sure, dear? It's been a heavy day." Even as she says the words, she passes my hand bag over my lap to my driver who takes it so I can get out with ease. She's learning quickly that I enjoy being alone when I can.

"I'm sure," I insist. "I will see you on Monday for our meeting with the Mayor."

As my feet hit the pavement, my driver offers her hand for me to take so I don't slip on the leaf covered sidewalk. There is a short shuffle as I'm handed my bag and we take the seven low steps up to my door.

"Do you need me for anything else?" the driver asks, still holding the umbrella high while I flip my deadbolt.

"No." I purse my lips, thinking. "But mark it as a full day's work with the service. Stay dry."

We don't exchange any more words as I slip through the heavy black front door. The dark painted walls and ceiling of the foyer greet me, looming over the space and the original 19th century chandeliers twinkle with warmth as I turn the lights up. On muscle memory alone, I set the alarms and relock the door. I place my purse on the sideboard by the door and step out of my heels, leaving them behind. Those are a problem for later.

The rest of my grieving widow costume peels away easily. The dress, the shapewear, the veil—all of the pieces follow me up three flights of stairs through my bedroom, until I step out the door onto the roof terrace.

This part isn't original to the house, but it may be my favourite. The cold concrete stones shoot pins and needles up my bare feet as I step into the rain. Surely I should be concerned about city pollution, but as I raise my face to the sky, I don't give a fuck.

I'm free.

Water drips through my hair, soaking my naked skin until I am covered in goosebumps and my body shivers in protest. Still I smile through the discomfort of it, just this once. I've spent six years learning to love my body for how it is, not what society thinks it should be. The weight that hangs from my bones is a gift. The brain in my head that brought me to graduate with honours is a wonder. My body is a trophy, a testament to the fact that nothing will hold me back.

Suddenly, there's a loud squawk.

It comes again when I don't do more than grimace at the interruption to my peace, this time sounding oddly like the blare of an ambulance. I look around and see a black bird high up on my privacy fence. Once it registers that I've seen it, it hops down and towards me, as if on a mission.

I've lived in Gwenmore long enough not to be scared of a single bird. Maybe a flock of pigeons is a bit creepy, or one of those rogue hawks the city introduced to keep the sky rats under control. That doesn't stop me from stumbling back when its tiny head nudges my ankle. Then I see a familiar crack along this bird's beak.

"Did you follow me home, sweetheart?" I ask. "Or has the rain just made me a bit stupid?"

The damned bird sighs at me. It nuzzles into my leg like it's trying to say "yes, I did follow you". The cold rain has frozen all my sanity. I grip the railing as I step down to the door into the house again. The bird follows me, hopping along like it belongs inside my home.

Absolutely not.

"Go find a tree, sweetheart, this ain't your house."

I'll stand in the rain all day if it means this thing doesn't follow me inside. I shake my foot at the bird until it moves far away enough that I can open the door and slip inside, then I slam it behind me. A shiver racks me as I'm met with the warm air of my bedroom. The heavy curtains cling to my damp skin as I press against the door. I know it's only the end of September, but I like a toasty house.

A coo and a peck by my side makes me scream. There is another, more metallic peck and I hear the deadbolt flip. My eyes widen as I stare at the bird perched on my door handle. How in the hell did it get in here?

"He-llo," it says.

Nope.

I am not having a single moment of this. I bolt down three flights of stairs to the kitchen. My phone is right there on the counter where I abandoned it with my hair pins. As long as that bird doesn't ruin my furniture, by dinner time I can forget it ever got in my house. Animal control will surely know what to do with a wild crow.

"Wait!" it shouts, clear as crystal as it lands on my phone, clawed black feet a stark contrast to the rhinestones and pearls.

This has to be some sort of late trauma induced by Jordan's death, brought on by the funeral today. That's the only reason I could be experiencing some Edgar Allen Poe-inspired mania. My breathing hastens, chest tightening. What the fuck is happening to me?

"Let me explain," it begs, voice mixing to something softer and almost painful.

I'm frozen on the spot. What can a bird have to fucking say? How can a bird speak, even? The whole "parrots echoing voices" thing is a myth, isn't it? Something Hollywood made up when they thought it was okay to abuse animals for the sake of a movie.

Oh, sweet Mary, mother of God, do not let this turn into a Hitchcock nightmare. I can't be Tippi Hedren.

The bird in question steps off my phone cautiously. The longer I'm still, the further from the device it gets, but it doesn't take its eyes off me until it falls off the counter. I lunge for the phone even as my cold body protests at the jerky action. My fingers wrap around it at the same time there is a bone breaking groan a foot away from me. Bile rises in my throat, and a painful chill runs down my spine.

From the other side of the counter, a dark figure rises. It's taller than me, but that isn't saying much. Wings, black and iridescent, elongate behind it until they span wider than my obscenely long kitchen island. The figure stretches for a moment, the shining metal spikes on the old leather jacket it wears catching in the low light of the room. My bottom lip trembles at the monster before me.

"Now." Its black beak opens just enough for the sounds to come out. "My name's Jackdaw Torrence, and we are fated."

My body and my mind finally succumb to the mania. The world spins and darkens, and the last thing I see is concern and fear in the monster's brilliant yellow eyes.

Carmela

34 Days

Everything fucking hurts. My head is pounding like I'm suffering from the red wine hangover of the century. Did I have anything to drink before going to sleep?

With a groan, I roll to my side. I plan to rot in my bed until the delivery driver arrives with the feast I'm about to order. Covers slip off my body, a shiver running across my shoulders before my hand jerks to a stop. Something hard digs into my wrist and I finally register that my fingers are tingling. I clench my fist a few times, but it doesn't ease the feeling. When I force my eyes open, I finally see the thick, leather padded cuff around my wrist.

This must be a dream from a shit sleep, because there is no way in hell I am handcuffed to my fucking bed. My gaze follows the cuffs to a black rope that disappears beneath the frame. Carefully, I rotate my other wrist and find another cuff there, as well. My eyes squeeze tightly together. There is a moment where I feel nothing. Not my body, not my bed, nothing but pure terror burning more than my muscles ever have.

So those letters weren't a lie.

Another reason I should have gotten a bodyguard instead of hiring Dotty. Hours after the reading of Jordan's will, a packet was delivered to our penthouse. No return address or postmark, just a thick legal envelope. Reception thought it might have been from my lawyers, so they brought it up. But when I opened it, it contained pictures of Jordan and his women, pictures of us out together, pictures of me going to get coffee or leaving my therapy appointments. They were creepy, but nothing that would cause damage. I didn't think anything of them.

A day later, I got the first letter. Typed and printed on cheap printer paper, there wasn't anything discerning about the threat it contained. *He wouldn't pay, but you will. I know what you did.* Still, I moved into the townhouse the same day and began calling around to local security companies to discuss optimising the systems in place here. Higher fences, motion activated lights, alarm systems—I had the full spectrum of private security upgraded or installed.

The letters still came, though. More pictures arrived, of me at St. George's funeral home, or speaking with my lawyer. The ominous threats quickly devolved into basic blackmail. Ten million dollars or they would tell the police what I did. Ten million dollars or they would hurt my new companion. Ten million dollars or they would hurt me.

No one should have been able to get into this townhouse without me knowing.

Baseless threats. Or so I thought, considering how little they were asking for. Being the face of a global tech superpower, his net worth was public knowledge. My refusal to pay was simply because I knew they would keep asking for more. They couldn't prove anything. The same way the police couldn't prove anything. Jordan died of *natural* causes. This was someone looking to make me feel weak and helpless again.

You're fine. Take a deep breath and feel your chest rise. Rise with it.

I exhale, and even as tears start to slip down my cheeks, I bring my wrists together to get a better look at what's being used to hold me captive. Despite the wide range of movement I have while bound, there is a small padlock on each of the buckles to keep me from just undoing them.

Next, I try the ropes to distract myself from the thought that whoever did this crept and snooped through my house. These were buried in the basement with Jordan's other things. I couldn't have it appear that I was erasing him from my life. Playing the part of the grieving widow is an important aspect of maintaining my image. However, I did spend the first week I lived in this house with a two-person cleaning crew removing every speck of Jordan from the house to the basement. That's how I know these are technically mine, because they belong to a set of bondage gear and other sex toys we found in a trunk in one of the spare bedrooms.

The cuffs are knotted together so tightly I can't even squeeze a fingernail between the loops. Hot, frustrated tears slip down my face and I scrub them away with the palms of my hands before I try once again, sitting up higher in bed like that will help me now. Everything was going so well. I was finally free of it all. I had the money. I should have paid the blackmailer and been done with the whole mess.

Desperation grows like a sickness in my chest. It seeps into my lungs with every quivering breath I take until I'm choking on it. My nail beds ache the more I try to squeeze one of my acrylics through the knot to loosen it. I have to get out of here.

I don't even notice the door to the walk-in closet open. The thought of checking my surroundings never once entered my brain when I realised I was tied up. My only concern was getting free. I should have checked, should have fucking remembered any of the self-defenses classes I took at high school.

A black, scaly hand with long razor-like nails wraps around my wrists.

A sob wrenches from my throat. I have all the fight in the world, but I can't make my body move as fear grips me. All I can think is that I was so close to winning, to having my cake and eating it, too. Through my tears I see a black figure sitting on the edge of my bed wrapped in a towel, and the mania I felt earlier rushes back. The panic, the terror that caused me to faint, all returns.

I haven't been tied up by a crazy blackmailer, but by a monster.

Its beak carefully tips up my chin while it keeps my hands restrained. Surprisingly soft, pale yellow eyes peer at me as though they have known me for a lifetime. There is a gentle rumble from the beast, like it wants to comfort me. It places my hands on its bare, damp chest.

"Sweetness," it whispers, in a low masculine voice. "Take a deep breath."

"No." I jerk, fingers digging into its soft feathers, pulling at them to hurt the monster. "Let me go."

"I can't. I won't lose you again."

"But you don't know me," I insist, before trying to bargain with it. "I have money. I will pay you."

It cocks its head to the side and rubs its scarred beak over my cheek. The texture sends a thrill down my spine. The grip the monster has on my wrists moves until it's holding both of mine with one hand and has them raised above my head.

The other sharp-tipped hand moves to my chest. The monster pulls the covers down slowly, revealing my bare breasts. Goosebumps prick across my skin at the chill, and my body reacts without my control. The creature doesn't grope me, or rip my beating heart from my chest. Instead, it takes one talon and swipes.

The slice stings. Blood wells up through the thin, shallow knick over my heart. I watch in horror as the monster raises its head and pecks its own hand. My breathing stutters as it presses its bleeding hand over the cut on my skin.

Then I feel it. Something dark curls inside my chest as the creature whispers in a language I don't know. My eyes flutter shut as waves of euphoria suddenly wash over me, relieving my sore body in a way I've never been able to achieve. My core tightens, and the moisture between my legs becomes undeniable as my mind is transported back in time.

There is a woman on a balcony. The vision skews, and it's like looking in a mirror. Her outfit is old, like she's just walked off the set of Wuthering Heights *or something.*

There is a book in her lap, and on the wide railing sits a blackbird. It lays a small, pearlescent pin before her, and she smiles.

The vision shifts suddenly to another scene, and I am standing by a piano, tapping on keys and the bird mimics them. There is a crash, and an older man bursts through a set of doors, shouting and chasing away the bird. He is speaking, but I can't hear what he's saying. This all feels too familiar, twisting my stomach into knots I thought I had untied.

These scenes of the bird and I keep playing out before me until one of them is dark, only illuminated by candlelight. I see a distorted version of myself on the floor, wearing a long white nightgown. Blood dribbles down this woman's nose, and she curls in on herself as the man from before reaches for an iron poker by the fireplace. As he raises it, the bird transforms, growing into the monster. Wings as black as the night tear through a great overcoat and the blood drains from all their faces. A beak that is smooth and polished catches the firelight before he attacks.

I witness the monster brutally murder the man, claws and beak working to tear out his insides and rend his flesh to ribbons. When it is done, the woman opens her mouth as if to shriek, but the beast tries to hold her. She runs, but not before grabbing a vase and hurling it at the monster.

"Your soul has found its way back to mine, sweetness,"

he murmurs. "The gods may have cursed my people, but we still have some magic. Do you feel the strings of fate now? How we are destined to be?"

Even as the denial is on my tongue, gossamer red threads lift from my chest to wrap around the bloody hand laying over my breast. They are met with dark and iridescent ones, twining together into a rope that doesn't begin or end before fading from existence. My lips part. I can't believe what I am seeing, and yet I know the monster is telling the truth. The facts are right here in front of me, but more importantly...

I *feel* it.

"Fortune has brought our souls together again," he murmurs.

Like he has turned on a light, I am suddenly aware of fate. There is no fear towards the monster before me. The talons that rest on my skin aren't going to tear through my flesh. The scaly skin that covers his hands and forearms is titillating. His body is covered in thick, black feathers that don't hide the muscles beneath them. They reach down to his knee joints, where his skin roughens again down to his feet, which are like that of birds.

He hovers over me, and yet I'm no longer scared. I'm curious more than confused by emotions rattling around in me. Something inside of me is telling me to lean into this, to follow that red little thread and entangle myself in the possibilities of what this monster is telling me. My heart pounds in my chest, saying only one thing.

Fated.

Like a memory of a love lost, I find that I want him more than I have anyone else. An undeniable urge to possess him, to never let him leave my sight again, takes hold of me.

That dark thing that curled inside me when his bloody hand touched me? It's burrowing into my heart and nesting right on my fucking soul. There is a well of emotions flooding my body that eclipses the pain and fear. His hand relaxes around my wrists and I follow him. My hands touch his damp chest over his heart, and I feel his rapid heartbeat stutter at my touch. They slip through his downy feathers, up until they are cupping the sides of his cheeks. His eyes flutter shut as though he hasn't been touched for years and that makes my chest ache for him.

"Please," he whispers. "Don't deny me again. I'll do anything for you."

His words stir the wretched parts of me that bloomed after I married Jordan. The greed, the wrath, the hunger for more and more, even when the world is at my feet. Hearing people plead for my husband's intervention changed me. I grew up in your basic middle class household and I got lucky by marrying Jordan—or so I thought.

But even with all the money in the world, I couldn't escape his controlling grasp.

Now this monster, strong and desperate, wants to give himself to me. Through whatever magic threads he has used to bind us together, I can feel his emotions, his submission to me. He is willing to give me anything, so long as I don't run in fear the way the woman in the vision did. I wonder what he'll say when he learns that I am just as much a monster as he is?

My fingers curl into his feathers and pull his beak down to my lips. I kiss the worn, craggy scar on it as he holds his breath. He's used my shower, but I'm not upset by that realisation. I can smell my soap on him and I like it. He wants to be surrounded by me, down to his pores. There is no part of my body or soul that questions this sudden connection.

What's a girl to do?

My hand snaps around the tip of his beak and he freezes. Those pale eyes are wide and staring at me with heat. The fingers still pressed to my chest curl ever so slightly, but he keeps his talons from digging into my flesh. I will have all the power here, and I will for the rest of our lives.

"If you ever tie me up without my consent again, I will kill you." I glare at him, watching my words settle into his mind.

A hunger forms in his gaze as the hand on my chest moves to the cuff on the wrist I'm using to hold his mouth shut. The long, black claw sets upon the leather cuff and slices it clean through. It falls between us and my fingers twitch as the tingling sensation eases. He quickly does the same to the other cuff, rendering both pairs useless. While that doesn't remove the threat of the rope, it's a start.

"Good boy," I murmur.

He moans, short and muffled, but I feel the vibrations of it. The sound stirs my core again, and I'm more than willing to test the boundaries of what anything means to my monster. If he likes being called a good boy, maybe he likes to play the submissive role in relationships. My hand on his cheek slides around his shoulders to his back until I meet the base of his wings. He shudders and presses into my hand, pulling me closer to him.

"If you want to be mine, you're going to have to follow my rules," I say, letting go of his beak to slip my fingers around his bare, feathered thigh. The muscles jump under my touch, but I don't look away from him. "I'll be good to you, if you are good to me. Does that sound fair?"

"Yes, sweetness," he says with a nod.

"Mm," I hum, smoothing my fingers over his wing. "When we are like this, intimate and vulnerable, I want you to call me Mistress. Will you, sweetheart?"

"Yes," he responds instantly, his voice rising in tone. It's not something I've been called before by a partner, but it heats my blood like I knew it would. I like the power he's giving me and even more the emotions flowing between are sizzling with matched desire. When I look at him sternly he quickly adds, "Mistress."

"*Oh*," I purr, fingers flexing and digging into him. "I like that."

"I want to please my mate," he reaffirms.

With the hand still holding his wing, I pull myself into a better seated position for this. My knees tuck underneath me so I am taller, more in command of our situation. His eyes latch onto my bare breasts and he swallows. His pupils grow in size the longer he looks at them, like he hasn't seen tits before.

"Let's start with a proper introduction. My name is Carmela."

"Mrs. Wisneiski," he mimics the words in Dotty's voice from yesterday, in her voice as if she were standing that same distance away shouting through the rain. I raise an eyebrow at him. "I'm called Jackdaw Torrence, but Jack is what I prefer."

When he tells me his name, I massage the base of his wing like I would a shoulder, and a soft moan falls from his beak. The sound makes my clit pulse. It's not feminine or masculine in tone, but a vocal partner in bed is delectable, a treat to be savoured.

I'm going to enjoy drawing every noise possible from him.

"Jack," I whisper his name as I lean into his shoulder. I take a peek at his wings, checking the base of them and how they tuck into his body. They are massive, and for some reason that knowledge makes me want him more than I already do. Perhaps I'm a bit of a size queen, perhaps whatever fate has woven us together is unleashing years of sexual energy. Either way, I've stopped questioning my wants. I'm in control of them again, and if I want Jack then I will do so however I please. "Let's play a game. I'll ask you a question, and when you answer me I'll keep touching you, pleasuring you. Do you like the sound of that?"

"Gods, yes Mistress," he whines when I press my lips to the side of his peak again.

"When was the last time you had sex?" I ask, keeping my voice low and sensual.

"Never," he answers quickly.

I pull back. "Never?"

"After I found her, I was content to remain in my bird form just to be near her. There are rules." He pauses as his voice breaks, the sound of shattering glass stumbling over his words. "And after she took her life, I vowed to remain alone if I couldn't have my mate. So no, I haven't ever had sex."

"Do you want to?" I ask. Jesus Christ, this has taken a turn I'm not exactly ready for. I wanted to make sure Jack didn't have any STDs, not take advantage of him. Because that's what I am doing, isn't it? Using his needs for my gain. I didn't feel bad about it before because we're consenting adults, but after a vow of celibacy?

"I can hear the nerves in your voice, sweetness." He tips his beak up and the lost hunger in his eyes has transformed back to the dark look from moments ago. "I'm not some innocent you're deflowering."

Even as the words come out his mouth in feminine tone, I hear them in Jordan's. The way he whispered them in my ear on our wedding night, how he revelled in taking my virginity, in the pain only he would get to cause me. My fingers on his neck tighten subconsciously, squeezing at where his jugular should be. I hate that phrase. I hate that word even, as if having sex for the first time changes a person, ruins them. A sneer curls on my lips and Jack's eyes sparkle as he leans into my grip.

"It was my choice, and now I am making a new one. Use me or don't, whatever pleases you, *Mistress*."

He looks at me for a long moment, not even blinking when my nails dig deeper into his feathers until I break the skin hidden underneath. Fabric tears as his talons dig into my bedding and my pussy throbs. I'm enjoying hurting him. Something wet twitches against my hand on his leg, and I take the chance to escape his intense stare. My gaze flicks down to his lap and the long, glistening exposed girth touches me.

Is that his dick?

It's like three rods fused together, each merging into the two ridges that make up the head of his leaking cock. The dark pink colour is dappled down the length before it turns a deep chestnut colour where it swells at the base. There is a part of me that is disturbed watching it pulse, but Jack's very existence has turned all the logic I once possessed upside down. If monsters are real, why does his dick have to be human like?

That is my mate's cock. The thought barrels through me, the word like a weighted blanket over my nerves. He called me his mate and thinking the same of him makes my heart beat faster, sets my blood pumping down between my legs until my clit throbs.

I'm going to be the only person to ever feel his cock, to know the weight of it in my hand and the taste of it on my tongue. The privilege of any knowledge is great, but this is precious—a gift he is giving to me as an act of faith or trust. And while I know virginity is a patriarchal lie, something about Jack giving me his makes me hotter.

"Do you want me to stroke you?" I ask.

"Please, Mistress," he whispers.

I take my hand and slide a nail from the swollen base to the tip. As my finger runs from one ridge to the next, his hips jerk and clear fluid drips from the slit. I tease the small bit of flesh between them and am rewarded with more precum.

"You're going to answer all of my questions before I let you come." I state the rule clearly. I'm not leaving this exchange without every ounce of knowledge this monster possesses. I can't read his mind, I just know that what we are feeling together is raw and honest. "Is that understood, sweetheart?"

"Yes, Mistress," he rasps.

Jack's body shakes and I finally soften my hold on his throat. He takes a deep breath, but leans into me like he can't stand the thought of being separated. His warmth is addictive and his body weight on mine is soothing, but I can't let that put me at ease yet. I need answers.

I push Jack until he falls backward, his wings spanning across the large bed and I mount his thighs. His hands move to my thighs, rubbing up and down gently. With both hands free, I wrap them around his shaft and squeeze.

"Are there more monsters?" I start my interrogation, watching more precum dribble out of him.

"Yes, all over the world. We have lived right under your noses for centuries."

"What is this?" I ask.

My thumb rolls into the seam of the swell at the base of his cock. That can't possibly fit inside anyone. It's massive.

"It's—" he groans when I squeeze it. "It's my knot, for locking my mate and I together for breeding."

His voice trails off into a whimper. My eyes widen at the thought of it. I can't be bred, but the stretch it would take to make it fit shots thrills down my spine.

I focus on the questions I need to ask immediately and try not to think about all the things that I could do to him, whether in pleasure or in pain. Still I wonder if that will fit inside me.

I stroke his cock, mimicking the speed at which he pets my thighs to tease him. "And what am I to you, then?"

"My Mistress, my sweetness," he groans when I clench my fist around the swell. "Your soul has been matched to mine by fate—*Gods* your hands."

His hips jerk beneath me and I let go. I will edge Jack to the end of the universe if that is what it takes to satisfy my questioning. His cock flexes as the pads of his fingers dig into me. My hands are sticky with whatever lubrication he's coated with, and I can't stop myself. I lick my finger carefully and find that Jack tastes like heaven. Our shared moan echoes around the room when I suck another finger into my mouth. He stares at me with wonder.

"Answer the question," I command. "Or I will punish you."

The feathers on his chest ruffle and I wonder how much pain he can take. Will he suffer beautifully for me?

"Many monsters have fated mates, and bird folk are the same. I believe you are a reincarnation of my mate, who was taken from me."

"There we go," I coo, returning to stroking his cock at a steady pace. "Can I trust you, Jack?"

"Forever more, Mistress," he promises.

We hold each other's gaze. I believe him. In this torrent of emotions and undeniable proof that something other than humans live among us, I know that Jack is telling me the truth even if it's just to get his rocks off right now.

My chest tightens as the weight of his words hits me. Soulmates bound together through fucking time, reincarnated to once again find each other when it's needed most.

"If I stopped right now and demanded you leave, would you do it?" I ask.

I need to know that I'm not shackled to him. For as much I desire to own him, to let him worship me, my freedom isn't going to be taken away from me again. I won't get stuck in another man or monster's grasp to be a pretty ornament for him.

"Yes," he whimpers. "As much as it will pain me to be apart, I will do whatever you ask, Carmela. Nothing will be too much. I will never deny you."

I hum a little and move my hands faster. For now that is enough. It's a promise I will hold him to, until my body is buried six feet deep. If this is going to be the start of anything, I need it.

Because I am not afraid to kill again.

"I'll see that you don't." I stroke faster, fucking my fist down onto his cock until the base as swollen to twice the size. "Now be a good boy and come for me."

The words are barely out of my mouth when he shoots off. The tip spurt ropes of cum across my stomach and chest. He is silent the whole time, his beak parted, but there is no sound of pleasure for him to mimic. I squeeze the engorged knot and more cum drips from the head of his cock. He doesn't know what it sounds like to hear someone in the rush of an orgasm.

We're changing that today.

Chapter Four

Jackdaw

54750 Days

My Carmela is as wicked as she is beautiful. Her sultry eyes stay locked with mine as my cum drips from her fingers. That little pink tongue lavishes her fingers where I can't. As the haze of my desperation fades, my thoughts snag on how different we are. I won't be able to kiss her, lick her pussy and taste her arousal at the source. Even with my hands, these claws are not made for gentle touches. They are made for tearing beasts and men alike to smithereens.

Still she praises me. "Well done, Jack."

It's a simple statement, something so everyday, but the purr in her voice and the low timbre of satisfaction makes my wings twitch. I never imagined my return to this city being anything but sorrowful. I would find that gravestone and then be exiled again, simply to have the punishment the council set out for me extended.

I won't let them take my mate from me this time. I won't let anyone take this gorgeous creature from me ever again. I will protect her with all my magic, all my abilities, all my life. Carmela is mine, and I am hers. A life of service to a woman such as her will be the greatest pleasure of my existence.

And I will do whatever it takes to please her.

"Mistress," I start, but I can't find the right words in my memory. Instead, a soft tearing sound like a letter being torn open comes out.

"Kneel," she commands, already shuffling off of me and toward the edge bed where she wants me to follow.

I roll off the side, soft cock finally sinking back into my sheath as I take a more submissive, worshipful seat before Carmela. Her plush body is on full display, from the tips of her painted toes to the flush on her cheeks. The city lights cascade through the windows of her bedroom and coats her in a pale halo of glory. Her body shines in its aura just like a jewel, and I am drawn ever closer to her. I want to possess her, but more than that, I want her to possess me.

She plants her hands on either side of her wide hips and spreads her knees apart. I draw in sharp breath, taking in the smell of her arousal. Moisture coats the lips of her pussy, the curls wet and shiny from stroking my cock.

"Look at what you do to me, Jack," she says. "Look how your pretty cock made me wet. What are you going to do to clean me up?"

More stuttering sounds leave my beak. Are my emotions written so plainly on my face that she could see my struggle? How am I going to please her when so much of me is too sharp?

"Give me your hand, sweetheart." She leans to the side and holds out her hand for me. It's much smaller than mine. My eyes catch on those glittery nails and a coo releases from my throat. Her smile is the true light of the night though. "Do you know how power exchanges can work in a relationship?"

"No, Mistress," I answer. I've listened to many audiobooks in the modern age, but none of them have sexual pleasure like what I've just experienced. The male narrator I like is always gruff and in charge when he's with the lady in those books.

"It allows us to be vulnerable about our wants and needs, and to get off on those feelings," she explains, her voice soft again as she smoothes a finger over the back of my hand. "I need to be in control, I enjoy when my partner lets me be in charge of our scene. Do you like when I'm guiding you, Jack?"

"Yes, even when my body is screaming at me to take over, I liked when you controlled me." My beak rests on her thigh. What more can I say to explain the exhilaration of her dominance over me? It never occurred to me how my desires could manifest this way. I want to serve Carmela, give her everything she could want even though she is a woman who clearly has it all.

"That also means we have to trust each other. I trust you to tell me when things become too much and you need to stop, just like I'll do the same. Do you want to stop?"

"No," I rush out, head lifting and shaking.

"Then trust me, I want you to touch me."

She kisses my knuckles before bringing my hand to her breast again. The smear of blood there is dry to the touch and she is soft underneath my palm. Her hand squeezes mine, the tenderness like a punch to my gut before she instructs me again.

"Now, play with my nipple, tease it with your thumb, pinch it between your fingers, until my pussy is weeping for your touch, Jack."

My body quakes with the weight of her trust. The gods have shined their light upon me, upon my mate, to bring us together again. My palm slides down until her brown nipple is caught between two of my fingers. Her skin is warm and pillowy as I grope at her tit. I do as she commands, pinching gently until her flesh is pebbled enough for my thumb to flick it back and forth.

At the first pass, her breath hitches. Hope begins to grow in my chest as I do it again, listening for a new sound. Her words of praise washed over me as she stroked my cock to completion, and now her pleasured noises drown all of my other senses. Little moans, the whimper that leaves her as I switch to tease her other breast, bring me back to life. I burn them into my memory until I know that my mimic will be perfect.

Her eyes flutter closed as she pushes into my palm and I take the chance to stare at her pussy, to watch her body clench around nothing, empty and begging to be filled. One day I will be worthy of burying myself inside her. When she learns more of me, when I have proven to her in all ways that our fates are woven together in the most perfect tapestry.

"Give me your other hand, sweetheart," she commands.

I react instantly, following her order without giving up her nipple. She hasn't told me to stop, so I roll the bud between my thumb and forefinger while she licks the pad of my other thumb. The blood in my head rushes to my cock again. My sheath pulls back and the head of the rods protrude like they also want to be licked. If that day comes, I will surely meet my end.

She takes my hand and places it over her mound, the curls teasing me. Her skin is warmer here, like a hearth calling me to nest in her. She presses my thumb against her clit.

"Do the same here," she says with a reedy breath. "Be a good boy and make your Mistress come."

She isn't concerned about my talons on her skin. They press indents into the curve of her stomach with each little roll of her hips into my touch. Carmela only wants her pleasure now, and she wants me to give it to her. My wings puff out behind me with ridiculous male pride as my cock starts to leak again.

My fingers move with precision that I have never known before. I have never touched another with pleasure in mind. Theft and trickery are second nature to me. In the past, my old love never touched me, and I was content with that for the rest of our days. I was content in being the bird she fed nuts and crackers to on sunny afternoons, and who tapped nonsense onto piano keys when I dared venture inside.

But now?

I will never know contentment if I can't touch my Mistress, pleasure her day and night at her command. Each of her moans grow louder as my thumb circles her clit. I can't take my eyes off the juices slipping from her pussy. But it doesn't matter, because I'm memorising each sound she makes, marking the placement of my fingers and what action they draw from her so there is no hesitation in my movements next time.

Her fingers curl under my beak, where the feathers meet bone, and pull my face up.

"You are such a good boy, Jack," she moans. "A natural at pleasing your *mate*."

"Carmela," I say her name in her voice, at a loss for anything more to say because I am moments for orgasm. My cock is untouched and yet it twitches where it drips on my thigh.

"That's right, sweetheart." Her voice is breathy, a current of urgency underneath her words. "I'm your mate, your sweetness, your Mistress."

A rumbling like that of a heavy truck over gravel rattles in my chest at her words. Yes, she is those things. She is mine.

"Yours," I pant. "Mate, monster."

All my words come out in different voices, but she smiles anyway. She doesn't care that I am cursed this way. Her body tenses and the world goes quiet except for the sound of her pleasure. Enraptured with her, I watch her lips part with ecstasy when she quakes in her release. Her body twitches like a small bird's would as she holds my stare, molten brown eyes burrowing into my soul.

My fingers slow, moving to hold her breast while my thumb sweeps through her cum to gather it all up. I don't wait for permission. My barbed tongue scrapes over my thumb and my hips jerk suddenly and pleasure rips through me at the glorious taste of her and our bond. Cum coats my feathers and there isn't a solid bone left in my body to keep me upright. I sink forward with only enough forethought to wrap my arms loosely around her.

We tumble back onto the mattress, my head resting on her soft stomach. I hear her heart pounding a steady rhythm and I truly believe I will be able to be happy again.

CHAPTER FIVE

Carmela

34 Days

I t's only once my stomach rumbles and Jack pulls my phone from the bedside drawer he'd hidden it in, that I realise I was out for only a few hours. I immediately look up the signs of a concussion and return to grilling my new toy for information. It's not normal to be passed out for that long, even if I woke up feeling like I only had a hangover.

"After you collapsed, I used some of the herbs hanging in your pantry to put you in a healing trance," he says, slipping his arms beneath my back again. He's still on his knees, his chest pressed to my wet pussy. "I know a decent amount of magic that is very handy for what I do for work."

"And what is that?" I ask.

A sort of chuckle comes from Jack and he looks into my eyes. "Professional thief at your services, sweetness."

"Ah, so you used your trade to snoop through my pantry and basement then?"

"Among other places," he says, eyes sparkling. "Your husband had excellent taste in leathers."

"I wouldn't know. Jordan hid me away like a broken toy when I didn't fit his ideal anymore," I say, picking at the rhinestones on my phone case. "This was his love shack, and I've been working to reclaim it."

Jack makes a noise of distaste and then pulls me into a seated position to look down at him. My hands go to his face, cupping his downy feathered cheeks. The warm light of the lamp makes the black feathers shine golden almost to match his eyes. He is strikingly beautiful, unusually to what I've always understood, and yet I want him again.

"Nothing about you could be broken," he insists. "Whatever makes you different, Carmela, doesn't make you broken."

"I can't have kids," I state flatly, trying to hide the guilt that Jordan spent years drilling into me.

"And? Your life on this plane is not one singular purpose to reproduce. Your value shouldn't be torn away from you until you are nothing but an incubator.

You're a being who contains multitude. One day, I will grow to love all of them if you will let me."

In my heart, I know he's right. I spent years in therapy working through the shit Jordan had done to me. He so efficiently infected all my thoughts, made me believe things that he wanted were my wants. Men can't be trusted, but I think I can grow to trust this monster.

Our threads, or whatever that astral crap was, have been woven together. Fate and free will are at odds with each other in my life, and I'm not sure where I should land on either. I'm walking a tightrope where no matter which I believe in, if I fall, I'll go splat.

"How did I get into bed?" I ask, changing the subject.

"I carried you, sweetness," Jack answers, flexing his arms around me as if to prove he isn't lying.

"Oh." I preen a little. I like the duality he holds within his actions. When he calls me Mistress, there is a vulnerability and power he's trusting me with. When he calls me sweetness, I can almost taste the freedom of it. That's something I can get used to.

My lips curl softly. "Then you're going to do it again. Draw me a hot bath. There are salts on the cart next to it. Add one scoop, then come back to me."

"Yes, Mistress," he says, voice cracking over the end of the word.

He slips from my bed and I let myself fall back into the soft mattress. His wings flex and swish with a dark wonder that keeps me staring at him until he disappears through the closet and into the bathroom.

The blood on my chest is crusty now, along with other fluids that are starting dry. I really did that. I stroked a bird monster's dick until he came all over me. There wasn't an ounce of real fear in me while I did it, either. Jack is different, and it will take some adjusting on my part, but as far as first encounters go with a sexual partner, he was damn near perfect.

This clearly isn't some one night stand situation. The way he speaks about us, about me, Jack is desperate for our connection to last. While I enjoy throwing a threat here and there at him, I don't want him to believe I would truly hurt him either. Not after what he has shown me, shared with me in blind faith knowing that I could handle it. I need to give him what he has given me.

Comfort.

"Jack," I call out.

The sound has my monster rushing back into the room.

"Sorry, it's taking a moment to fill up the tub." He looks ready for me to reprimand him and now my emotions are just as messy as my body. I don't like this look on him. Do I sound that horrid after an amazing orgasm, or is there something else on his mind?

"You alright?" I ask gently, sitting up on my elbows and looking at him.

"I don't know," he says quietly, as though the words are getting lost in the wind. "I feel...off? I've felt grief strong enough to kill a man and I have survived a long time, but..." He drags his claws over his chest while he searches for a word he can't articulate.

Something emotional stirs in my stomach. Tiny whispers of my therapist's explanation of aftercare filter through my thoughts. There is a difference between being in control of someone and being a bitch. Right now I feel like a grade-A bitch for not having a real conversation about boundaries, and letting the power he's given me go to my head.

"Jack," I say, beckoning him closer. He crouches down until we are face to face once more. "Do you feel unsure about where we stand? About what's happening between us?"

"Maybe?" he offers. "Do you feel unsure?"

He says the words back to me in my own voice, and I hear my hesitation. This is otherworldly and new. Humans don't just get soulmates out of the blue. But despite it all, I find I'm not scared of the future when I look into Jack's golden eyes.

"Yeah, in the same way I'm unsure about what we're gonna eat for dinner, I guess, but I know I still want it. Just like I still want you."

There is vulnerability in my voice, but I take his hand in mine anyway. What has happened, has happened. We can't change the past, but we can control how we act in the future. I used to think of that cliché shit when I was planning to get rid of Jordan. Every time I ignored the moaning coming from within my own home, I just thought a little harder about what it would sound like when he was dead, planning my reactions to the police and the media and everyone else.

I guess it's really a cliché because it applies to all sorts of situations. We can't change what led us here, but we can take steps to make sure things go right. Communicating our needs and feelings is a goddamned cornerstone for a healthy relationship.

"I don't know what will happen tomorrow or in a year, but I know I want to at least try to make this all work." I smile a little. That therapy shit is good money spent.

Jack nods and slides a talon across my hand. For some reason, I think he is smiling despite the beak.

"I will relish the chance to work on our future together, sweetness."

"Good," I say. "It's probably a good idea—"

His head cocks to the side. "Bath's done."

Then he moves. His arms slide underneath me and those great black wings spread curl around me as he lifts me off the bed in a swift motion. *Jesus Christ.* I grab onto his shoulders for stability as he cradles me in his arms. His warmth wraps around me as he takes me toward the bathroom. Surrounded by him, I can smell more than my shampoo. There is something subtle about the way he naturally smells that makes me want to snuggle in closer. I don't know what it is, but it makes me feel settled.

The steam from the bath smells warm and herbal. He's picked my favourite bath salt without even knowing it. Carefully, he lowers me into the large bath, soaking his feathered arms again. He gently gathers my hair and twists it atop my head with a clip before easing me back to lay down. My chin just tips under the surface when I speak.

"That's the stuff," I sigh, pressing the button on the control panel to my left. The jets come to life and my body relaxes fully. "One thing about me: I live for little indulgences like this."

Jack shuffles from his crouched position to sitting on his knees, laying his arms around the edge of the tub. "So finding you pretty jewels will not win me any brownie points?"

"Maybe a few," I tease. "But what can I do for you?"

"You're perfect the way you are." His voice shifts accents as he speaks. "Carmela."

When he says my name, he says it in my voice. I narrow my eyes at him. Why does he do that? He speaks so smoothly that the odd sounds and effects in his voice are barely noticeable most of the time.

"I will have to find an audiobook with your name in it," he answers my silent question. "My people, a long long time ago, were cursed to be like this. Our voices were stolen and our human forms ripped from us by the gods. We thought we were better than them, and they proved us otherwise. I don't even remember what I used to sound like I've been this bird creature for so long."

"That's awful." I turn my head so I can look at him fully. "So how do you speak, then?"

"I have a very good memory, and can mimic nearly any sound I hear." To demonstrate, his beak parts and a sound like paper ripping comes out. "Very handy that audiobooks have become so widely available."

"Do you have a favourite?" I ask.

The feathers at the top of his head rise as a stuttering sound comes out of him.

"Are you embarrassed to tell me?" I press, but he only nods. "Why? You shouldn't feel anything negative about what you enjoy reading. Cringe is dead."

"Have you heard of the *Wildemaw* series? They are a set of fantasy historical romances that follow different couples, but they get the same man to narrate the main male character for each book. He's also done a few action thriller books, but—" he clears his throat before he finishes his confession, "—I like happy endings. I used to think I would never get one."

"Happiness is never guaranteed," I say. "You have to work for it."

"I will work for your happiness for the rest of our days then, sweetness," he says. "What else do you want to know?"

We stay like that long into the night. I press the heat cycle button whenever the water gets too cool and Jack drags in a chair from the dressing room as our conversation flows from small to big talk. His feathers slowly dry, turning fluffy under the low light bleeding in from the closet. The longer he sits, the more his body tenses as if he is struggling to control himself. He fidgets in his seat, his tail feathers flicking and his wings rotating up and down as he crosses his legs once again.

"Are you okay?" I ask.

"You are very beautiful," he states. "And while I'm very much enjoying our conversation, my body demands release."

My eyebrows raise. Monster libido sounds fucking intense. I hum a little when an idea comes to mind, and a fresh, seductive smile forms on my lips. His honesty and straightforwardness makes me happy. I don't want either of us holding back. I spent too long doing it and I won't again.

"How do you feel about cockwarming?"

Carmela

34 Days

The two best things in life are chocolate covered strawberries and orgasms. And with the infinite wealth I gained when I got married, I still never made them a priority. Years spent focused on male pleasure and cooking dinners have ruined me in many ways. I am making efforts to change that, which started with having a supply of chocolate-covered fruits sent to my house once a week. They arrive every Thursday, and by Saturday afternoon they are usually all gone.

"Are the ropes really necessary, sweetness?" Jack shouts from the couch.

"Are you uncomfortable or horny?"

He lets out a long grating sound like groan, and when I look up from creating my platter masterpiece, his head is thrown back. The length of his body extends in one long black line from the tip of his beak to the claws of his feet, which curl into the Persian rug. Jack's cock is hard and glistening against the feathers on his abdomen, while his hands are loosely tied behind his back.

The open plan design of the house never appealed to me until now. There is a good ten feet between Jack and I, but I can clearly see how desperate my new plaything is. I lean against the kitchen island and watch him huff for a moment longer. It's dark outside the window, the only light coming from the electric fireplace on the far back wall. The red glow plays with the highlights of his feathers, making them burn.

My body pounds with heat and anticipation. When I explained our scene to him, the little idea I had, he jumped to untie the ropes from the bed. Excitement coursed through him as he practically hopped down the stairs, long wing feathers grazing each step.

As the ropes slid through my fingers and gently around his arms, a softer warmth enveloped me, like I was in control of our fates. I was the one tying us together this time, instead of the forces of the metaphysical. Each loosely-tied knot connects us again, cementing us together in this time. Our lives are twining and knotting together so quickly and so easily.

With my platter of fruits and cheeses in one hand, I pick up part two of our scene. The heavy silicone dildo has been scrubbed clean and is only slightly smaller than Jack's cock. I'm not about to hurt myself by taking the real monster between us without a little stretching, and I do believe this will work both of us up even more. It's a pleasure to know there will be no jealousy between my little bird and the toys necessary to help us work.

Before binding his arms, Jack moved the furniture around in the living room, shoving the coffee table to the side and moving anything at risk of being knocked over by his wings against the wall. Now all that's left is the narrow, vintage saddle bench. At the time, I couldn't tell you why I wanted that piece of furniture, but now as I attach the dildo to the harness strapped to the bench, I feel like it was fate. The sky wizards knew I was going to have to erotic explorations with a monster who liked to submit to me.

"From now, I only want you to call me Mistress," I instruct. "And if for any reason we need to stop, we'll say so, got it?"

"Yes, Mistress."

Jack already sounds a bit weak for it and it makes my pussy throb. With the tray off to the side, I move to stand in front of him. The silk robe I'm wearing is more to keep me from flashing the neighbourhood than to keep me warm, but the curtains are drawn. This space is all our own now. The outside world doesn't exist, there is only us.

"Untie my robe," I command.

There is a slight jerk in his shoulders, like he's already forgotten he can't use his hands right now. I cock one eyebrow at him and he coos. Slowly Jack grabs one long end of my robe with his beak and tugs it softly. As silk does, it slips apart and reveals my body to him with ease. I let it fall from my shoulders before I cup the underside of his beak and kiss the scarred top.

"Good boy," I murmur. He shivers under my grip and his wings twitch against the back of the couch. "Don't hold anything back for me. Voice your thoughts by any means you need to."

"Yes, Mistress."

I turn and am instantly met with another grating groaning noise. "Is there a part of you that isn't perfect?"

Heat rises in my cheeks as I walk the three steps toward the bench. I want to be close enough that he can see everything in detail, but with enough distance he can't reach me. As I straddle the bench behind the harness, I adjust the nylon straps, making sure they won't slip when I start fucking the toy. The dildo comes up to about the curve of my stomach, but it's the vision of Jack's cock that makes me wetter. That is my goal, to be able to sit on his cock and tease him up close with ease. I want to feel the knot at the base of his cock swell before he fucks it into me, and it *locks us together.*

"Gods you are a gorgeous, Mistress," he moans.

"Are you always one for compliments, Jack?" I tease.

"For you, Mistress. I'd rather spend my days in silence than hold in my thoughts about you."

"Flattery." I smirk, sliding a finger through my labia to bring some of my arousal to my clit. "It'll get you far, sweetheart."

A sound like glasses knocking together comes from Jack. His eyes are glued to my hand as I circle my clit. My hips slowly start to roll as my nipples tighten in the warm air. The longer he stares at me with that hunger in his eyes, the hotter I become and the more I want to toss aside the scene. My pussy aches to be filled.

"Don't come without my permission," I demand. I'm not sure if he can come untouched easily or on command, but he did earlier when he tasted my cum. I want him to save it. Some delusional part of me wants to make sure he fills me with so much cum that it never stops dripping out of me.

"Of course, Mistress," Jack promises in a whisper.

"Are you ready?" I ask.

I rise up on my tip toes and hover over the dildo, smearing my wetness across the head as I line myself up. Jack doesn't make a sound, his beak parted slightly, and then I hear the very soft slip of silk sliding across silk. It's almost too quiet to hear and I only recognise the noise because I just heard it.

My hips lower slowly, teasing us both while my pussy stretches easily to fit the toy. Jack makes a choking noise when I'm fully seated. His body jerks upward, cock ignored and beginning to leak across his feathers. My pussy flutters with pleasure.

"Gods, fucking hell," he moans, his accent taking on a interesting lilt at the curse words. "I can feel your pleasure, I'm so fucking hard just watching your little pussy sit on that cock."

"Do you want me to ride it?" I grin. "Show you how I could be bouncing on your dick?"

"Please."

I plant my hands behind me and move at a slow pace. The angle drags the head of the dildo across the front wall of my pussy, teasing the spot behind my clit. My nails dig into the leather and my thighs grip so hard I'm going to have harness marks on them, but I lose myself in the task. Watching Jack's feathers ruffle as he breathes harder and harder only increases my desire. His eyes never leave my pussy, enraptured by the sight of it swallowing the toy.

The coil of need in my abdomen winds tighter and tighter the longer I rock. My orgasm builds steadily under his watchful eyes, and I wish his hands were on me. I crave the feel of them grabbing hold of me, sharp talons teasing my skin. I want the danger of his power while he submits to me. The rush of our first sexual encounter fuels me. My weight shifts to one hand as I massage my clit, jerkily swirling my fingers around it.

"Jack," I keen.

"Please, Mistress, show me how you'll come on my cock," he begs.

"Fuck," I shout, moments later. My thighs shake, knees giving slightly as my body jerks. I keep moving my fingers, forcing my pussy to clench and grab tight on the toy.

Panting, my body limp and loose, I slide off the toy and fumble around the harness until I've got it unstrapped. There is a soft haze in my thoughts, a wild abandon as I present the silicone cock to Jack. He stares at the fluid clinging to it before he looks up at me.

"Clean up your Mistress's cock like a good boy, sweetheart," I command.

He doesn't hesitate. His beak opens and a sharp, hooked tongue carefully takes the cock into his mouth. Our eyes lock as he lashes the toy with it, groaning at the taste of my cum in his mouth. My body begins to burn the longer he ruins the toy just to get a taste of me. His wings spread further out, his shoulders rotating, and I know he wants to grab hold of me. The rope doesn't creak though, and he doesn't try to get out with real effort because he submits to me first.

"There," I say, stroking the side of his face to signal to him that's enough. "My good boy."

Jack leans back, inhaling through his nostrils and squeezing his eyes closed. There are small, shallow cuts sliced through the silicone now. It doesn't disturb me as I look at it. Receiving oral pleasure isn't something I require from a partner, but watching Jack destroy this toy for a taste of me has given me many ideas for the future. It's awakening a different side of me that I didn't know I possessed.

"Say something mean," he says suddenly.

"What?" I blink.

"I'm gonna come."

"No, you won't," I state. "Because you have better self-control, Jack. And you don't want to be a bad boy for your Mistress, do you?"

"No," he whimpers. I look down at his cock and see it throb, a small pool of precum staining his feathers. "Meaner, Carmela, make me submit or I'm going to ruin your carpet."

It takes me seconds to decide if I'm into this side of dominance play as much as I am watching his eyelashes flutter when I praise him. I drop the harness and grab hold of his beak like I did hours ago, jerking him to look me in the eye.

"Don't be pathetic," I hiss. "You've made such a mess already, like a needy slut who can't stop himself. One taste of my cum on plastic and you're ready to blow your load?"

"I'm sorry, Mistress," he mumbles, hips thrusting between us at nothing.

"Maybe I should just leave you here all night for being so easy, cock hard and leaking."

He shakes his head, and I feel a ragged breath stutter out of him. His cock twitches again, but his hips don't move. He takes another breath and I smooth my hand to cup his beak.

"You were very quick with that," he says, a pleased sound in his voice.

"Better?" I ask. "Not too far?"

"Just the right amount, though. I like the idea of being your needy little whore." He preens softly as I scratch the area where bone meets feathers.

"Next time." I grin. "Are you ready for more, or do you want to be untied?"

"Use me as you see fit, Mistress."

I move the forgotten tray of fruits to sit next to Jack on the couch. He settles in before I climb into his lap. The brush of feathers against my soaked vulva tickles and shoots pleasure through my limbs. Every brush of our bodies together stimulates some part of me, electrifies all my senses in a way they never have been before. The previous incarnation of me was a fucking idiot for not jumping on this when she had the chance.

Jack should have had a long life with that version of my soul, but it was taken from him. I'm not going to let that happen again. Right now, with my fingers wrapped around his cock and twelve hours of being tied together, I know I won't let anything untie us. I will spend as much money as I need to make sure we are given the chance we deserve, fate be damned.

Our bodies both react when I slide the head of his cock through my folds. My clit throbs at the tease of its tip pressing around it. Each little twitch of his muscles acts like a set of lips mouthing my clit. Next time, I think, next time I'm going to tease us both with this. Jack turns his head slightly when I slide the tip to my entrance, keeping the point of his beak away from my face.

"Eyes on me," I whisper.

"They always have been."

That first press into my pussy doesn't stretch too wide, but as I slowly lower myself I feel it. My muscles grip the thickness of his cock and pulse the deeper I take him. Seated at the base of the swell, I'm shivering, unable to stop how intense it feels and how much pleasure is coursing through my body. His knot is wide enough that as I roll my hips, it rubs against my clit.

"Fuck," I moan. God, this feels good. Jack's body is tense beneath me, his breathing ragged. This is both the best and worst idea I think I've had in a long time. I curl my feet up and over his thighs to add balance to our position.

"This is…" his voice breaks with the sound of a dog growling. "The most exquisite torture."

"Imagine what I could do if I really wanted to hurt you," I murmur, digging my hand into the feathers on his chest right over his heart.

"I believe you're capable of great violence, sweetness."

If only he knew.

His bright yellow eyes glow in the low light. His body is hard and lean where mine is soft and full. Jack has spent lifetimes alone and in sadness, and I've only lived enough of mine to know I wanted away from people. We are opposites, and yet twin flames drawn to each other by some kind of otherworldly force I wouldn't have believed in two days ago. He is being sewn into the fabric of my soul just by being near me, and I can't risk him being ripped away too soon.

He's my secret until I figure out how we are going to survive together. When my blackmailer realises I won't give in to petty demands and pick a new target, then I'll find somewhere for us to go. Maybe a cabin or whole island, anywhere but here.

"May I feed you, Mistress?" Jack asks. When I don't immediately respond he adds, "I promise you'll like it."

I know exactly why I am wary of this, but I nod anyway. He has been willing to try for me, and I want to reciprocate. Jack leans over to the tray, eyes flicking back to me before he selects a chocolate covered cherry. Every little shuffle makes my core clench around his shaft, but he doesn't say anything. He presents the fruit to me, held at the very tip of his beak.

He's a cheeky thing, my monster. With my messy hand, I cup the underside of his beak and bring it towards my mouth. He holds his breath, eyes locked with mine.

"You've been thinking about this, haven't you?" I ask, my lips brushing over the chocolate.

"Yes, Mistress."

"My lips wrapped around you, kissing you, teasing you."

Jack's cock twitches and it lights my body up. My breath hitches in the back of my throat. As cool as my attitude is, my body is wound tight. There are no more words when I finally take the fruit. My lips close around it and Jack's beak as I pull the cherry free. His eyes burn into mine when I crack the chocolate coating. Sweet and tart burst in my mouth and I groan.

"Fates," he whimpers. "I won't last. The things I want to do to you, Mistress. I am a beast."

"But you're my beast, Jack," I say, leaning over to grab another piece of fruit. "I will bring you to heel as many times as it takes."

I lick the chocolate strawberry slowly from base to tip before I take a bite. His cock flexes inside me once more, knot pulsing against my clit. When I'm finished with one, he grabs the next. The mango slice drips juices down his beak. I watch it slip to the feathers before I take the chance to lick him clean. A shiver vibrates up his body when I take the fruit this time and shoots pleasure across my core.

The weight of him inside me is maddening and centering. Each flex of his cock makes my pussy pulse tighter around him. We are connected as closely as we can be. It's intimate and soft, even as we fight to keep our carnal needs at bay.

It's perfect.

Once the tray is done, both of us take turns to feed the other before we're panting. My pussy is soaked and relaxed while Jack's knot has grown even larger. It presses into me, but never slips inside. The sensitive tips of my breasts shoot fire right to my core with every brush of his feathers. I am tired and needy to the point I've haven't corrected Jack the last two times he hasn't called me Mistress.

"Just say the words, sweetness," he coos, the rumbling from early in the day returning as his beak brushes the side of my neck. "I'll take over and fill your little cunt just like you want."

"Damn those fucking audiobooks," I curse. "I need to find this author and thank them."

He rumbles something, a noise I can't understand, but I sense it's an agreement. When Jack's cock flexes again, my clit can't take it anymore. It's too much teasing. I've pushed myself to the limits of overstimulation and I need to switch roles. I make a noise, a sound that is wholly pathetic but even in my own ear makes me hotter.

"Let me take care of you, Carmela," he whispers. A part of me breaks inside. I had everything I could have wanted. I still do, but am I going to accept what I need? To have somebody care for me without restraint and without expectation, that's all anyone wants. It's just taken me so long to find someone I trust to give it to me.

"Please, Jack."

I fumble for the loose end of the rope and with a quick tug, the bindings loosen. His shoulders droop and roll before he slides his arms out from behind. He's careful as he gathers up the rope and sets it next to the tray. I try to watch, try to be an active participant and match this otherworldly stamina, but I can't.

My thoughts unravel like loose threads on a sweater. I tug on one, thinking to tease him or ask him a question, but then they come undone. Cushions are tossed on the floor and I must look confused enough for him to explain.

"I'm making a nest."

I giggle a little, and then a lot when I'm lifted into the air. Jack's cock is still hard and buried inside of me when he brings us into the makeshift nest he's made in front of the fireplace. The rug beneath my back is lush and padded, and tomorrow I'm sure I'll pat myself on the back for picking this one out, but all I can do is stare up at how beautiful my monster is.

Jack's feathers glow against the fire in a beautiful array of oranges and yellows that match his eyes and remind me of setting suns, or the last burning light of a hot summer day. He's a warm vision of the future I hadn't anticipated. I tell him as much, but he just chuckles a little.

"When I returned to the city, I expected nothing but sadness to greet me. But then I saw you, sweetness," he whispers, cupping my cheek. "And for the first time in over a hundred years I felt light, hope. You are my future."

Jack grinds his hips into mine softly. His wings spread out and drape over the cushions around us. Speckles of light break through them and dance across our bodies.

"I won't let us fall apart," I promise.

It's too soon to make any sort of pledge like that, but I can't stop myself. The words that tumble out of my mouth are honest, straight from my pounding heart.

"You are mine, Jack."

"For as long as you'll have me, sweetness."

At long last, he pulls his hips back and we both shudder at the change. When just the tip of his cock inside me, he pauses and takes a steadying breath. I run my fingers through the feathers on his arms, squeezing the muscles there until I can cup his face.

"Fuck me like you mean it," I whisper. "Like every time could be our last. I don't want to leave anything unsaid or untouched."

He turns his head just enough to meet my gaze before he nods. With a hand planted next to my head, he wraps the other around my back and raises me up to put me in a better angle to take his knot. My back bows and knees come further apart to make space for us both.

"Your body is as beautiful as your soul, Carmela."

I want to call him the same, but the words are lost on my tongue when Jack starts to move. His hips drive forward, filling me to the brim. My mouth falls open, but no sound comes out. Jack holds my body in place as he does it again. Each thrust brings a quiet gasping sound from me. I am dazed and oversensitive. My pussy grips onto him every time he pulls back. I can't bear the idea of being empty again. Not after we spent so long as one.

"Jack," I moan, a needy noise following suit.

"Come for me, sweetness," he pleads. "I need to feel it, please."

"Harder, show me the monster."

He snarls, some noise that is nothing like the ones he has made before. The hand next to my head curls into my hair and he leans back just enough to get a better look at me. His gaze is sharp, cutting me to the core as his actions don't match up. His claws are soft, a tickling sensation on my soft skin as he brutally begins to fuck me.

This time I shout. My body blazes with something darker as he finally lets himself go. He uses me like a toy, plunging into me with abandon. His knot pushes harder and harder against me, each clench of my pussy another chance it will finally sink into me. A litany of words come out of my mouth, none of them making sense with sounds Jack makes to match.

I reach between us to rub myself. I need to come, I need to come so my monster will force his knot inside me. It's the only thought I can muster as I pinch and circle my aching clit. Jack doesn't falter. He holds pace as our bodies slap together in a wet mess.

A thread of clarity breaks the surface of my ravenous desire. The edge of my orgasm is there and I find my voice just before I tumble over the edge.

"Be a good monster, sweetheart. Knot your mate."

There is a final slap of our bodies meeting as his knot slots into me. It stretches and swells the walls of my pussy, pressing behind my clit as it pulses until we are coming together. My pussy contracts and I cum, fluids gushing around us. Jack throws his head back, his beak open, but doesn't make a sound. My legs shake and my fingers tremble in their hold on him. Jack curls over me, his body jerking with each surge of his climax.

"Mine," he whimpers as he holds our locked bodies closer together.

"Yours," I whisper, hugging his body to mine.

We collapse as the sun starts to peek through the edges of the curtains, our limbs tangled together and Jack's wings draped over us like a blanket. We fall asleep holding onto each other like lovers who are finally reunited.

Chapter Seven

Jackdaw

54751 Days

My wings flex under the warm sun penetrating the windows, and I awaken to the sense of my body being explored. Light touches brush over my beak, and delicate fingers smooth down the feathers that cover my chest. If I were somewhere else, my first instinct would have been to slash their throats. Years alone and wandering have hardened me. No monster could get that close to me and live to tell about it.

But I could never forget finding my Carmela, of falling asleep with her in my arms. Sometime after my knot slipped free and my cock returned to its sheath, she woke up and used the bathroom. Instead of going off to bed without me, she dragged a large blanket from the couch over to our nest before curling into my body and falling back asleep.

I pry my eyes open and see she's been awake much longer than I have, as she's also opened all the curtains. Her robe is back on and next to her sits a new spread of food and drink. I don't linger on what the particulars are because my sweetness is trailing her nails over the rough skin of my hands.

"Morning," she murmurs.

I make a croaking noise, happy to leave words out of it while I take the chance to bask in my mate and the sunshine. Yesterday started so grey and wet, but this morning everything feels fresh. Fortune has come to me in sways and I want to writhe in gluttonous euphoria.

"How are you feeling?" she asks, wrapping her fingers in mine. There is a touch of vulnerability in her voice that I don't understand. Fate has brought us together, yet we are still strangers, twisted and knotted together. There is so much I have to learn about Carmela that I can't from our bond.

"I feel like my life is finally starting," I tell her, wanting to be honest without bearing all the wild emotions floating around my skull. I have to work up to those, and build a strong foundation to prove my devotion. "Is it odd to say thank you?"

She smirks, the corner of her full lips lifting just enough as she huffs, "No. I just wanted to check that our scene yesterday wasn't too much. I'm new to that kind of sexual dynamic too. And our...other dynamic?"

"Mates?"

"Is that a common thing?"

"Yes, but what we do with the connection is our choice." I squeeze her hand, but when she doesn't continue speaking more words flutter out of my beak in a fit of nerves. "I know what I want, but what do you want? Now that we have the fresh light of day and calmer minds."

She pauses for another moment, and I wonder if she will tell me to go. I would do it. I would leave her house, but I don't think I could bring myself to leave Gwenmore knowing she was here. I would let her live her life, but I'd still be there in the shadows, a bird flying from gutter to wire to lamp post while watching out for her. I know I'm not strong enough to abandon our connection. Humans can forget and move on, and if Carmela does, I will live through the torture of it, but I can't leave.

Her soul is the only one made for mine. In whatever form it takes, mine will find it.

"I realise I said some things that may have been very emotionally intense," she starts, never letting go of my hand. "I haven't been in love for a very long time, and I'm not yet, but given the space, I would like to try. My ex-husband did a fucking number on me, and I'm not sure I'll be able to trust men again."

"Then it's a good start that I am no man."

Carmela's laugh is husky and short. She lets go of my hand and I move to sit up.

"I meant what I said yesterday as well," I tell her. "You can trust me, and I will do whatever it takes to earn and cherish that faith."

There is a twitch in her brow, and the set of them tells me she wants to question my allegiance more, but then her stomach grumbles. She smooths a hand over it and reaches for the tray. There are tiny crackers and vegetables surrounding a container of hummus, with a jar of cornichons and snack cakes next to it. Does she always graze this way?

"Can you eat gluten?" she asks before I get my chance to quiz her.

"Yeah."

"Interesting," she hums. "Birds aren't really supposed to eat bread and stuff."

"Well, I am not really a bird, and I don't have a cloaca," I point one clawed finger at her before I stab a carrot with it. "Do you always eat picnic style?"

"I haven't cooked since Jordan died." She smiles, a soft blissful expression on her face. "It's been nice."

"Jordan Wisniewski." The name rings fire alarm style bells in my head. That human was well-known and rich as a king. I hadn't connected the last name to Carmela because he was twice her age, and she mentioned being married for a while. "Sounds like a cunt."

She chokes with laughter, nodding and coughing at the same time. She takes a large drink of orange juice and sighs. "Surprised I was married to him, aren't you?"

"Well—"

"Everyone thought I was so lucky to snag a billionaire. I haven't spoken to my parents in almost ten years because of him. He moved them to Mexico after we got back from our honeymoon, then he started picking away at my friends. One by one, there was a new reason I couldn't hang out with them. Soon, he was all I had, and he wanted nothing to do with me anymore. I was stuck in our penthouse apartment with everything and nothing all at once."

I swallow the lump in my throat. My sweetness is reliving the past in her own way. It was common then, in her previous life, to be trapped in marriage. I never expected to see it now. Her ex is lucky to be buried before I made my return to Gwenmore. If I had met Carmela while he was alive, I'm sure history would have repeated itself in a perfect carbon copy.

"He had two skills, computer shit and manipulating people," she continues. "But I don't want to talk about him, Jack. Tell me about you."

"I'm an open book, sweetness. Ask me anything."

"Did you like killing that man?" She picks up a broccoli stem and swipes it through the hummus before she pops it in her mouth like she's asked me my favourite dessert.

Carmela cuts right to the quick. The vision she saw during the ritual didn't leave out any details. She knows what I did, and yet still had the bravery to grab hold of me. A shudder ripples through me, and I puff out my feathers thinking about how she first touched my beak. The anger in her soft features, how her tears evaporated when she saw she could get the upper hand. My cock threatens to reveal itself, but I reign in my need for now.

"Yes," I answer honestly.

"Good."

Later when Carmela is freshly showered and waiting for more food to arrive, she runs out of questions to ask me at last. I have followed her from room to room as she pointed out things she likes, quizzed me on monstrous history, and told me scraps of information about herself. She's a quick one, my mate—intelligent and wise at once. She's hesitant to share her past with me, but I know that will come in time. We are new, and for as well as she's taking the real world being revealed to her, I know that fate will throw challenges at us.

"Do you want to stay in Gwenmore?" I ask, watching her glittering nails tap on the kitchen counter.

"Maybe. I don't know. I've never really lived anywhere else."

"I would happily take you anywhere you'd like to visit," I murmur, taking hold of her hand so she knows the only thing I'm tied to is her. "This place hasn't been my home for a very long time."

She hums, a noise that I have come to realise means she is thinking very hard about something, debating whether she finds my answer suitable. She doesn't need physical things from me. This house, the town car from yesterday, and the labels on the men's clothes hidden away in her basement are a testament to that. But her wealth doesn't mean I can't give her the intangible: happiness, adventure, and love.

I want all those things for our future.

"Where has been the best place to—" A low doorbell tone drones through the house, interrupting Carmela's question. "That'll be food. Can you get the chilli oil out of the pantry?"

She points to the door by the dishwasher before running up the stairs. This house still has the original floorboards, so I hear every creaking step even when dampened by the thick carpet. The pantry is small but well lit. There are jars and jars of things stacked in neat rows. A vast collection of herbs hang from the pegs on the shelves.

The large deadbolt on Carmela's front door unlocks, and all my feathers bunch up. Not in all my years have I seen a house with so much security. Perhaps I was never stealing from the right crowd. It's much easier to grab a phone from a man in a business suit or snatch a wallet at night when people are too drunk to notice.

Or maybe I made the right choice, because I was never caught. Who's to say now? I grab the chilli oil off a low shelf and as I rise up again, my beak catches something on a shelf and mail comes toppling down around me.

Letters and photos are scattered across the tiles. It's a suspicious hiding place, but I barely know my mate. I try not to think too hard about it, and respect her privacy considering our odd start, but then I see the lewd photos of a vaguely familiar man with a woman.

They are not photos of Carmela, not at first. But then I find others, pictures of Carmela and the same man. He must be Jordan, and these are photos of her dead husband with all his various women. Then, I spot a photo of Carmela speaking to someone in a dark parking lot.

I look at the papers next. They are threatening letters, demands for crazy amounts of money are spewed across page after page or else What could she possibly be hiding that is worth so much to this person? Has she paid them already? Do I need to protect her? If someone wants to hurt Carmela, they will have to deal with me.

And I'll kill them before they even get the chance to harm her.

No one will take her from me. History can't repeat itself, I won't allow it. I gather up all the evidence, intent on performing my own interrogation, when a vase shatters. My blood runs cold and my heart rattles in my chest. It's a noise I would recognise anywhere.

Carmela's house is elegantly laid out and decorated with care. I spent quite an amount of time snooping through her belongings, trying to learn more about her before she gave me her tour. While the floors are the same as they were all those years ago, she has transformed it. She's shown me how she's made it hers, so she can finally have a space of her own. She wouldn't break something so clumsily. Images flash through my mind of that night a hundred and fifty years ago. The fear that haunts this house has awakened again.

I transform before I can think better of it. The pages flutter back to the ground and my small body is flying up the stairs. I look at the mess in the hallway and the foyer, a shattered vase and Carmela's broken phone lay next to each other.

She's not here.

CHAPTER EIGHT

Jackdaw

54751 Days

The back of the Ravenscroft Somnium Library is just as grand as the front. The classically-designed columns stand tall. A tall fence surrounds this portion, creating only a narrow alley space for employees to smoke or take a moment for themselves. The old doors that used to be another entrance are sealed shut, and cameras are posted at each corner. Under each window, a large flower bed is bolted into the stone that makes hopping up and peering into them more tactical.

I don't know if the boogeyman will recognise me after all these years. I don't even know if he will be here, but Deg'doriel will have told him by now that I have returned. The council are protective of the city, of this home they built and now control. A vagabond like me returning will not go unnoticed, and I can only hope they will help me before deciding my new sentence for once again mating a human.

At the next box, after rows and rows of ornate bookshelves, I arrive at an office. This room is jammed full of books, with an overstuffed chair near the window and a fine looking jacket hanging from the tree by the door. It must be Augustine's.

"Just like that, mon abeille," a voice growls from inside the room and as I press closer I see the nightmare sitting in his chair behind his desk. His glasses are off, eyes as black as the sands that pour from his skin and float around him. There is a whiplike snap and then a feminine moan.

"Your lips were made for pleasuring my quills, Joanna, shaped by the fates to serve me," he groans.

While I never thought of Augustine as the type to form amorous connections, it seems I'm destined to suffer his wrath for disturbing this one. I stab my beak into the glass repeatedly until the pleasured sounds stop. My eyes are closed tightly until I hear the click of the window unlatching and sliding open.

The boogeyman glares at me in his monstrous form. Spines of glass, forged from his sands, rip through his back, and his golden hair is dishevelled as veins of sand pulse under his skin. He stares down at me, and tendrils of darkness float around me, waiting to strike and suck the aura from my body until I am nothing but a husk.

"Help me," I beg. "Please, Ravenscroft."

His lips peel back and reveal sharpened teeth, a grotesque grating sound vibrating through his chest.

"Augustine?"

The woman from under his desk speaks softly and I avoid casting my gaze in her direction. Whatever manner of monster she is, it won't compare to the threat of the one before me. Especially if I anger him further by invading their privacy.

"Please," I say again.

"Get off of my flowers, Mr. Torrence."

"Who are you? Ow!"

The noise of his guest in pain strikes fear across Augustine's face. I have never seen this look on him before, and over such a short noise. In his hurry to check on his partner, he leaves the window open and I take my chance. I enter the room as he surrounds the short, nude, mouse-like woman now standing behind his desk with his sands. Again, I make a pointed effort not to look as I transform to my full height.

"I need your help," I insist, voice cracking like dry branches falling from a tree. "My mate has been taken from me."

"Your poor ability to—"

"Augustine," the woman chastises him in a way that reminds me of an old mated pair. She clearly has no fear of the monster she's enthralled. "Give us a second."

"Mon abeille, you do not even know this beast."

"Yes, but *we* are old acquaintances, Ravenscroft," I cut in. "And I have served my time."

I won't tell him my new mate is as human now as she was then. He may hold knowledge of reincarnation within his sands, use them to break my connection with Carmela's soul, and I can't risk him severing our threads. He can only be trusted so far. I will use Augustine and his connection to the council to track down my mate, and then I am taking her away. We will never return to this city again, and will live our life in the peace we deserve.

There is shuffling behind me, the telltale sign of clothes being put back on in a rush, mixed with the same grumbling noises Augustine used to make a century ago. It seems the fates are looking upon me with some grace today after all.

"Torrence, was it?" the woman asks, and I take that as my prompt to turn around.

Her round features relax into one of shock when she looks at me. She leans forward and presses her elbows into the desk. Her clothes are unlike Augustine's, under-tailored and a bit drab. In fact, when I look at her now she seems his visual opposite, and yet the way his sands cling to her shoulders and twist around her hands tells me their relationship is more than just a fling.

"I prefer Jack," I say.

"What are you?" she asks next.

I blink and look at her with a touch of shock. One of the many social queues of our society is to not so bluntly ask what sort of monster a being may be. It's considered rude by most, and many monsters can sense it. We can smell or feel what sort of magic runs through a being and use it to discern what they are. Even now, I sense an odd freshness to the power shining through her. It's not quite right, but not quite wrong, either. If she can't sniff out what I am and she's not old enough to know about the plight of my people, she must be...

"Human," I snap, gaze zeroing in on Augustine as the betrayal, the double standard of his action, makes me lose sight of my purpose here. "You—" My voice cuts as the sound of breaking glass takes over, and my beak aches with the phantom pain. He has a human for a mate, too.

"You have been gone a very long time," he says carefully, my unguarded emotions revealing to him how confused and desperate I am at this moment. "These are new changes for us all."

"My mate has been taken from me," I stutter out, trying to shove all my chaotic emotions down. The ache in my bones at being separated from my mate again, at my control being ripped from me, is threatening to spill over. Our tapestry was just being set, the threads beginning to weave the story of us together. I can't let this new revelation overshadow it.

"Then we will find her, Jack," Joanna promises with utmost certainty. "We understand what you're going through."

I look back at her and see sadness in her eyes. What horrors has this poor human seen to give her a look such as this? Is that what is to become of humans once they learn of us? They realise that those of us who lurk in the shadows make the world all that more terrifying?

Carmela didn't have this melancholy in her eyes. The more she questioned me, the more comfortable she became. She knows I would never hurt her, and that I am hers. If she never wishes to know more, I will not force this world on her.

But my promise to protect her tore so easily.

"When was she taken?" Augustine asks.

"Not even an hour ago. She was expecting a delivery and went to answer the door. I found threatening letters in her pantry, so someone was clearly after her. I had no idea."

"Does she *know*?" Augustine asks.

"Yes, it's been a whirlwind the last twenty-four hours, Ravenscroft. Can you do anything?"

"Are you sure she did not simply run away?" he asks.

"Carmela wouldn't." I know she wouldn't run. She'd kill me first before trying to run away. I can feel her grip on my beak from yesterday, see the fire in her eyes when she threatened to kill me for tying her up.

"Okay, okay," Joanna says in a soothing voice. "Jack, why don't you go back home, then we will call some people and convene there?"

"It's the same house as when we last met." I look to Augustine. "She was taken from there once, and now history seems to be repeating itself."

"She is still alive, Torrence? Surely you can sense that?" the sandman insists.

Can I?

My mind's eye can't seem to break through the fog of fear and confusion that clouds it. I can't see where the threads of her souls lead, just that they are far enough away. How can I have let this happen?

My body crumbles back into my small form and I fly away, back to her home. The window is still open, the vase shattered on the floor. A wail seeps from my chest through my beak as my body transforms again. We were just reunited. I can't lose her again.

I kneel in the shattered evidence around me. Dread laps at my thoughts, even as I take stock of everything around me. The side table has been shoved hard enough to scratch the wall, several of the rhinestones are missing from Carmela's phone, and a letter is jammed into the mail slot of her door.

My beak clicks when I stare at the white envelope again. That wasn't here earlier. I collected the post this afternoon while Carmela was getting ready. Gingerly, I grab hold of the unmarked paper and tear down the short seam with one claw. My blood boils as I read the note.

366 W Penn Drive

Come or she dies

My finger flies across my phone screen as I type in the address. It's in the new suburban development to the west of the city. I drop the note for the others to find, if they come to help me at all. I must bring my mate back.

Chapter Nine

Carmela

35 Days

Calm is not the emotion I thought I would experience in the face of my blackmailer. If he ever showed his face and tried to make good on his threats, I figured it would be an adrenaline-fueled fight to the death, not a fucking kidnapping from my own house. Why take me to a second location?

Does he know Jack was there?

While he erratically drives through Gwenmore and into the suburbs west of the city, I remain the best damn captive he could ask for. At each traffic light, each time we sit still for longer than a minute, his frantic energy grows. He doesn't ever honk his horn though, or shout at the cyclists cutting him off.

But his fingers tap on the gun in his cup holder.

My hands are zip tied together, the plastic digging into my wrists painfully. Nothing like the padded leather from yesterday. What the fuck has my life become that I'm fondly remembering being chained to my bed by a different stranger? Jack's not exactly a stranger anymore, though.

Mate.

It's an odd term that's growing on me the longer I sit here. Truly, whatever late stage trauma has bound me to that monster only seems to grow tighter and tighter around my heart. I think of the loveless marriage he wouldn't let me leave and trapped I felt every time he would remind me I was his *wife*.

But as I play back my few short encounters with Jack, that same caged feeling doesn't come. He called me his *mate* and it felt good. His impulsive and quick response to destiny has brought nothing but pain to him in the past, and yet he dove head first into it again. He doesn't deny where fate guides him, either. He seems to flutter along.

Perhaps I should have listened to fate more, but where would that have gotten me? Certainly not here, but it would have been worse in other ways. Would I have met Jack if I never killed Jordan? I don't think I would have had the confidence to accept a monster if I hadn't first known what darkness lied in me.

Taking a person's life changes you in some ways, and in others you remain the same. I still believe glitter nail polish is superior and I still enjoy a good Neapolitan slice. But I'm not blind to what drives people. The greed and power that so many of Jordan's peers were desperately clawing for disgusts me. The ways he lorded it over them as if he were a god himself just made him all the weaker in the end.

He wasn't so powerful when I stood there and forced him to drown in his own vomit. At first, his eyes were filled with anger at my dinner making him so violently ill. It was one thing he never complained about, the one thing I was good for anymore, so to get it so wrong was a cardinal sin in his eyes.

That little mix of herbs in his chicken really did wonders to create a food poisoning effect.

When I shoved his weakened face harder into the bowl of the toilet though, his fear vibrated through his body. He scrabbled and fought for a while, but he was still trying to throw up the poisoned herbs I gave him. His body was too weak to overpower me. Still I held his head submerged for three minutes after he stopped moving.

I would do it again just because I could, but also to have this new world revealed to me and to meet Jack again.

My eyes close as I think about him. I know he'll find me. If the vision we shared and our time spent together this weekend have proven anything to me, it's that he won't lose his mate without a fight. And he was a killer before, will he kill again for me?

The car jerks to a stop outside a plain house that blends in with the others around the street. It's quiet, but there are cars parked in several of the driveways. If this guy shoots me, people will hear it.

"Get out. Let's go," my blackmailer barks.

He jogs to open my door, but before he does it, there is a pause and I know he's looking around the same way I did. "Don't fucking scream."

"No, no, wouldn't want to bother anyone with a fucking abduction, would I?" I sneer, awkwardly shoving my way out of the car.

The man doesn't say anything, just grabs hold of my arm and yanks me the final distance out. I try to measure the odds of me versus him right now. He's taller than Jack is, and built hardier, but around fifty years old. The lines around his eyes and mouth and the grey in his hair make me think he is the same age Jordan was. They look so similar, too. That's probably why he's so hung up on being owed a portion of Jordan's estate—maybe he is a distant relative to my dead husband.

"Hey, hey, I don't have shoes on, so watch the damn rocks."

"Shut up," he hisses.

"And if I don't?" I challenge him. I'm not scared of what he'll do right now. He dragged me out of my house in my pyjamas and zip tied me, but he radiates fear. Maybe if he breaks open an old car battery to drop acid on me I'll be scared. Right now, I'm fucking annoyed and he left his gun in the car like an idiot. All he can do is hit me.

"I'll... I'll..." He growls some stupid noise when he can't think of something scary enough. It's only then I wonder if he's a monster. Jack said they were everywhere. But if this man were a monster, why not just attack Jordan years ago? He claimed to be sending him letters too in his first threat to me. Blackmail feels like an impressively human action when there isn't extraordinary violence to back up the claims.

Already, I can think of ways I would have done this better. My blackmailer drags me into the house, and its sparse furnishings are old and worn like they were new when the house was purchased twenty years ago, but they haven't been treated with care since. There are no toys for kids, no pictures on the wall, no shelves of books or movies. This place is a shell of existence.

He takes me into the kitchen, of all the rooms. There is a small table and chair by an oversized window and I'm told to sit there. He paces around for a moment, pulling out jars and a coffee maker. I recognise some of those herbs as he starts dropping them into the filter.

Shit.

"So how did you know Jordan?" I ask, swallowing to ease the sudden dryness in my throat. I need to keep this facade up, pretend I'm not bothered.

"That ungrateful bastard," he grumbles, hands gripping another jar too tightly as he shakes. "Stole my fucking idea. It should have been ours."

"Ideas aren't a one and done thing." I roll my eyes. "You could have had more."

He grabs a knife from the block and points it at me. "Don't patronise me."

"Jordan had loads of ideas." I keep talking, though, because if he comes near me with that knife, I'm gonna kick his nuts so hard his eyes cross. "Yours probably wasn't even the best."

"Do you know who I am?" he suddenly asks, returning to dumping more herbs into his coffee filter. He's gonna put me in a coma or kill me with that amount. If he's trying to make the same mix I used to make Jordan sick, he's doing it all wrong.

"Not a fucking clue," I say, leaning back in the chair and crossing one leg over the other. "Clearly not someone successful or smart enough."

The man stops. His movements freeze mid-air like a cartoon's until he raises his eyes to me. They are dark, deadly, and familiar. It's a look I've seen in the mirror so many times. He may not have been willing to hurt me before, but now he won't hold himself back.

He rounds the table, knife pointed at me. In the span of a few minutes, I have turned this kidnapping up to a level I'm not sure he was prepared for. I pushed the right buttons at the wrong time. This is why I'm not impulsive, why I plan and wait until everything is perfect so I have full control over these situations.

The knife slides right through the meat of my thigh, tearing the muscles on the outer edge of it. I didn't think he had it in him, and I was proven wrong.

The world flips and twists, and bile rises in my throat as my legs jerk and fall apart. It's a burning, searing pain that I can't understand. My hands shake and refuse to grip the space above the knife. Blood wells up around the wound and slowly trickles down. My gut is telling me to pull it out, take the pain away, but I know if I do that I will bleed faster.

My kidnapper's eyes widen as he stares at the knife, like he can't believe he just did that.

"First time?" I ask, tears trickling down my face. "Hurting is hard, isn't it?"

"What?" His voice is almost a whisper. He can't stop staring at the blood. "What do you know about..."

"What do you think I did?" I goad him to try and understand why he's been blackmailing me. It's the least he can fucking do if he's going to watch me suffer. My voice rises as I try to keep the pain to myself. "Why did you do this?"

"I know you had Jordan write me out of his will," he states, eyes flicking back to my face for only a second.

"I don't even fucking know you." I grit my teeth. For Christ's sake, this fucking hurts. How long is Jack going to fucking take? My heart thuds harder and harder in my chest, and I swear I can taste blood now.

The man stumbles back, a hurt look striking through his face. "I was his goddamned brother."

"Jordan didn't have a family," I counter. At least, that's what he told me. He was an only child, his parents died shortly before he graduated college, and he had no aunties or cousins to console him. He was all alone in the world.

"This look like fucking family?" the guy shouts.

He turns his back on me. There are seconds for me to do this, to rip the knife out of my goddamn leg and stab him. There is no point in being quiet. There is no point in pretending I'm anything but a monster to him.

I yank, a scream tearing out of my throat and my vision blurring. The shape of him turns back, but I lurch forward. There's no coordination, no plan. I fall into him as hard as I can knife-first. He grabs hold of my arms, but there is a sickening, squishy feeling to whatever part of him I've punctured, like preparing a pork dinner but the meat is underdone. There's resistance, and then he just gives.

When we fall backwards, the knife drives so deep into him, the handle pushes into through his ruptured skin and blood spills faster than before as the seal around the blade breaks. I don't think. I roll off of him and take the knife with me. My kidnapper gurgles for a moment, but then he is moving, too. How is he not fucking dead?

"Carmela!"

A shadow falls over us, a pair of massive wings blocking out the bright kitchen lights before they retract just as quickly. The metal studs on his leather jacket catch the light so prettily. I blink away tears as Jack comes into view. The blood-soaked knife slips from my trembling fingers as he eases me up to sit against a table leg. He grabs hold of my wrists and cuts the zip ties with his talons.

"Shit." I wince as blood flow returns to my hands. I hadn't even noticed they were so uncomfortable.

His hand smoothes over my face, down my neck. He looks so worried for me and so scared. The feathers on his head are puffed up, and it makes me smile. He looks ridiculous. Maybe it isn't funny because of the ongoing crisis we're in, but fuck am I just glad he's here.

A broken glass sound trickles out of him when I run my hands over his beak.

"I need a towel, and then we can finish this," I instruct Jack.

He scrambles around the kitchen, ignoring the man bleeding out against the refrigerator. Seeing his blood-drained face and the terror in his eyes, I think he might be telling the truth about being Jordan's brother. They have the same look about them when they're close to death.

"Where?" Jack asks, fists full of tea towels.

The burning in my leg finally takes hold of me. I grab the towels and press them where it hurts most. Every breath I take is heavy, and I can't make my heart stop pounding. Fuck, does this hurt, and there is so much goddamn blood.

"Jesus Christ," I groan when Jack applies more pressure.

"You're going to be fine, sweetness," he says, like he's promising himself that more than me. "The bleeding will stop."

"Of course it fucking will, but fuck me."

"I have friends coming to help."

That should ease my mind, but it doesn't. The fewer people who know about this, the better. We can't brush a kidnapping and murder under the rug if more people see the evidence. That's too many wire transfers to keep straight.

I take a few deep breaths. My leg throbs with a burning pain and the rest of me aches in response, but I'm fine to keep moving and keep up appearances.

"We need to kill him before they get here," I explain. "We have to tell them he's lost his mind, took me from the house, and it was self-defence. There's something on the fridge. Give it to me."

It's really not a lie, but our stories have to be similar enough. There can't be any evidence that this guy is connected to Jordan in a meaningful way. I don't know who his friends are or who they are connected to. I'll pay off the coroner again to falsify a report. They were willing to do it once, I'm sure they'll do it again. Times are tough.

Jack does as I ask. When he steps near my kidnapper, making a sound like a chainsaw before plucking the paper off the refrigerator. He doesn't react to whatever it is, but brings it to me. It's a photo from about thirty years ago, and shows two men in a small, shitty closet of an office smiling at the camera with a server rack behind them. They look almost identical.

He flips it over. *Jordan and Chris, Ski Tech's first lab.*

"Chris," I call out.

"My own fucking twin," he whimpers. "Going to change the world, and he cut me out at the first chance he could."

"He was a manipulative sack of shit." I groan, saying the same thing my therapist told me years ago. Some people are just users, and won't give anything in return. Jordan was just very good at hiding it, even from his own brother.

"I just wanted my share." Chris' voices wavers. Maybe he's not as alive as I thought, and this cover up will be a bit easier. "We shared everything."

Jack pockets the photo and looks at me. He's ready to kill, but he won't until I say so. Power over a man's life is a fine power to have. I hum, brows furrowing as I think about what I should say. My monster, my mate. Should I trust him?

"You'll still get to share everything." I nod my head at Jack, who walks back over to the fridge. He doesn't pick up the knife I dropped, just crouches by a trembling Chris. "I killed Jordan, and now I'm killing you."

There is a gasping sound when Jack shoves his finger into the brutal knife wound. I watch, morbidly fascinated, as he wiggles it around. Moments later, blood dribbles from Chris's mouth and he begins to choke. Jack removes his finger and rinses it in the sink like he's just spilled sauce on it rather than shoving it into a man's guts.

"Can you drive?" I ask.

"No, why would I need a car?"

My eyebrows pinch together. That makes sense, why do you need a car when you can magically turn into a bird? Are his friends, who are apparently going to be here at any moment, also bird people? Is anyone going to be able to take me to fucking hospital? Without my phone, I can't even call Dotty to come and get us. I'm not putting weight on my leg or even attempting to get behind the wheel after this fucking day though, so we are going to sit here with this dead guy and wait.

Jack dries off his hands and looks out the window over the sink. He coos a noise of surprise, almost like wind chimes softly blowing in the wind. He starts rifling around in the cabinets, and when he doesn't find what he's looking for, he runs out of the room.

"Still here," I mutter, as he leaps over me and Chris.

There's more rustling, sounds of doors being opened and closed throughout the house. I lean my head back, still holding blood stain towels to my leg. I look over at Chris, his lifeless eyes meeting mine. I really do see the resemblance now. Jordan hurt so many people to get where he wanted in life, and even more just because he could.

I don't have any more tears to cry. Not that I would cry them for a man who blackmailed, kidnapped and stabbed me. The strings of my heart don't tug for anyone but Jack, and seeing him bounce back into our crime scene with a folded sheet and a bottle of peroxide makes me smile.

"First aid has arrived, m'lady," he chirps.

"Oh, no." I chuckle. "I'm not mated to someone who sincerely says *m'lady*, am I?"

He makes a canned gasping sound, like something he's heard from a C-grade movie rather than the audio books he likes. As he tears stripes off the sheet, I watch his arms flex under the tight leather of his jacket. I like the cut of this on him, but I'm finding the more I look at Jack, the more I just like looking at him. The late afternoon sun is still so warm, and every once in a while his feathers reflect a dark rainbow of colours.

"I haven't done this in a while," he admits. "Should I call 911 or something?"

"No, too many questions. We have to deal with this ourselves and I'll pay for others' silence. I don't make a habit of getting stabbed, so hopefully this will be the last." I smirk. "Let's get this over with."

With my approval, Jack works like lightning. I'm doused, dried, and wrapped up in a neat package before I can think twice about the use of chemicals on my wound. That's a problem for the doctor to handle when I call him later. Fuck the hospital now. They don't need my minor injury blocking up their waiting areas when I can call a private doctor.

Jack opens the back door to the house before he comes back to me. "Let's wait outside and enjoy the sun," he says.

Before I am even finished nodding, he bends down and lifts me up bridal style with my injured leg held away from him. The jostling makes it throb, but he's trying so very hard to be gentle with me. His talons nip at the silky fabric of my pyjamas while his warm palms press into my soft sides and hold me closer to him. Beneath the smell of my soap on his feathers, I can just sense the warmth and musk of Jack. He still smells like me, but it's becoming the smell of us.

Out in the backyard, there is a patio, a fire pit, a circle in the grass where there was once a temporary pool, and a stone bird bath. The bird bath is so ornate that it looks odd amongst the rest of the suburban aesthetic back here.

Next to it, there is a lounge chair. It's well-placed, like Chris used to spend hours out here thinking about ways to make Jordan see him, and later, make me see him. Now he won't see anyone and I don't feel bad about it. As far as I'm concerned, the end of the Wiz Kid and his evil twin brother is a boon for this city.

Jack carefully arranges me in the chair before he runs back into the house. I close my eyes for a moment and feel everything that has happened in the last twenty four hours, the last month, and the last decade of my life, all of which have landed me here. I feel the weight of the loss and the insanity of it all. So many chance encounters, of fate in action, brought me to this backyard.

But I feel free, like this chapter of my life has finally ended. Jack and I are starting a new one together.

A blanket falls across my lap and I open my eyes. Jack balances a platter in one hand while he fusses about making sure I'm tucked in. Then he presents his creation to me.

"Freshly washed," he promises, a knowing tone echoing after his words.

There are slices of banana, chilli crackers, protein bars broken into pieces, and a small pile of sour gummy worms. Couldn't ask for a better meal if I wanted one. I pluck a piece of protein bar off the tray before Jack sets it down to balance on the bird bath.

He cups my cheek, talons weaving through my hair until he can scratch my scalp. My neck and shoulders soften under the touch. I want to close my eyes and drown in the feeling, but I can't take my eyes off him. His breath ghosts across my face, shaky and uneven.

"I thought I lost you again," he whispers. "I was so scared."

I wrap my fingers around his wrist and press his palm into my cheek so he can feel my pulse, the warmth of my skin. We are both alive and real. The world is filled with monsters, but the being before me is nothing of the sort. All I see when I look into his yellow eyes is a lost soul hanging on by threads of hope, just like I was. Our threads are stronger knotted together.

"No, sweetheart." I smirk. "You're stuck with me now."

It's a promise. We are partners in crime, accomplices to a murder, and soulmates. Our fortunes and follies are woven together now. Fate may have torn us apart in the past and brought us together now, but we are going to write our own future as one.

Chapter Ten

Jackdaw

0 Days

Her laughter echoes around the fire pit as I attempt to sing an old cowboy song I heard once. It's more of a rickety croaking than a chorus, but the joy in her eyes is everything to me. Carmela lays her head on my shoulder, snuggling in closer as a chill rolls in with nightfall. We should have called for an ambulance, but she was insistent that we wait. She doesn't want to have to explain the dead body or speak to the police.

"If your friends are coming, I'll just pay them until they can't refuse."

So I built up a fire while we waited. There was enough ash in the bottom of the pit to make me believe Chris did this pretty regularly so there isn't much concern about neighbours thinking it's suspicious. He seemed like such a sad sack of shit, all alone in this house trying to blackmail his own godsdamn brother into caring. Still, I'm glad I could make him suffer even for a moment for what he did to my sweetness.

My hand lightly runs over the makeshift bandage. She's stopped bleeding, but I'm anxiously awaiting the arrival of Augustine. Carmela's soft sigh does nothing to ease the worry weighing on my chest. I made her eat all the food I brought out earlier to help steady her, but now I'm concerned she hasn't drunk enough water.

Instinctively, I wrap my wings around us to protect her.

"Such a pretty boy," she murmurs.

"What?" I ask, but then she tugs at one of the spikes on my jacket. I stole this off a drunk punk decades ago. A good, busted leather jacket was hard to come by, and what can I say? The shiny adornments drew me in.

"You don't seem like the type of hard ass to wear studded leather," she explains.

"My ass is very solid," I joke. "Pert and spankable."

I mimic the sound of a clap and she hums, causing my feathers to twitch. Already, I love that little noise she makes. I don't want to call all of my feelings for Carmela that yet, but the first threads have been laid. As we weave more into our story, the emotion will be undeniable. I don't doubt it or question it.

My wretched soul knows hers divinely.

A soft click in the distance has my head twitching in that direction. Someone unlocks the front door and a number of footsteps creep through the house. They aren't dampened by sands like the last time I awaited these monsters. Instead, I hear the click of wooden soled shoes and the squeak of sneakers.

"Oh shit," one of them squeaks.

There is a quick exchange between them, but I focus on Carmela. She has started to doze off and as much as I wish to leave her undisturbed, something is telling me she would rather be stabbed again than sleep through this.

"They're here, sweetness," I whisper, smoothing my beak across her cheek. "What would you like to do?"

"Stand behind me."

She moves even as she gives me the command. A look comes over her face, stone cold and dripping with privilege. Her silken pyjamas are blood stained and her hair is tied back with a rubber band I found lying around the house, but my Carmela looks like a boss. Nothing about the way she looks affects how she holds herself now. Without a sound, she crosses her injured leg up over the other so she is positioned sideways in the lounge chair. Ever so casually, she leans against the arm for support.

I take my stance behind her and off to the side so if I must react quickly there will be nothing standing between me and them. I tuck my wings in tight and hold my head high. My stomach curdles with anxious anticipation, but I know for certain that no one will tear me apart from my mate tonight.

I refuse to let fate repeat the past. For as long as she lives, for as long as she will have me here, I will remain by Carmela's side.

The first person out of the door is Joanna, the human. She's wearing a strange all black tracksuit and her face is ashen. We probably should have covered up the body, but I can't say I give two fucks for that guy. She grips her nose, but when she sees Carmela her mouth drops open.

Augustine fills in quickly behind her, followed by a flash of purple. Deg'doriel either isn't scared or is putting on a show to test my mate. Either way she doesn't react to him. From here I can see he looks...tired. Like something inside of his festering and he can't find a cure. Kragnash comes last, or I assume it is the disgraced highborn because that war dog of his is still by his side.

From the corner of my eye, I see Carmela swallow. That is the only tell she gives as the beings who are to help us come towards our fire pit. Covered in blood and bathed in firelight, my mate is a gorgeous creature. She is meant to rule an empire and to be by her side while she does is a gift from the gods.

"Now this is a surprise, Nash," Carmela says first.

The large white man with grey hair smiles, revealing a golden tooth. Like the orc so long ago, his casual attire makes him look like your average human, but I can see the quality in the material from here. The shine on the buttons of his sweater reflecting in the fire light. He touches his hand and magic flashes through the air to reveal the orc I remember.

"Mrs. Wisniewski," he says.

"That's not a name I answer to anymore, Nash." She smirks before turning her gaze to Augustine. "Mr. Ravenscroft is it?"

"Have we met before Ms...?"

"Carmela is fine, and no we have specifically, but I did write you a rather large check seven years ago to fund the renovations on the library. There is a computer lab or something dedicated to my late husband."

The sandman's cheeks darken ever so slightly. Not in a sense of anger, there are no pulsing black veins, but with embarrassment. What happened seven years ago? Does my sweetness know the details or is she simply dropping loaf size bread crumbs about her connections with the high society of Gwenmore.

"The Wiz Lab," Joanna mumbles. "It's really popular."

"Thank you, honey," Carmela says. My wings twitch under the sweet endearment. I don't like it and she must have felt my movement because my mate hums that note again. She's deciding whether she found my response acceptable. "I'm happy to hear it, but honestly I don't give a rat's ass."

"Look, are we done here?" Deg'doriel asks. "This is gonna be a long fucking clean up job with Arlo at work tonight."

"Then by all means, leave Grimace." She looks down at her nails as if that isn't a very powerful demon.

"Carmela Maria De Marco, I baptised you once, and I'll fucking doing it again with force—"

"Fuck," she curses. "Father John?"

"Deg'doriel," he says. "Or Doug."

"Does this mean I'm not catholic anymore?" she asks.

"What does anything mean anymore?" the demon laments. "You mated a human again."

When he points his purple finger at me, a hellish flame dances on the tip.

"She has the same soul," I state. "And is clearly taking this all very well."

"That doesn't change the fact you broke the rules again, almost instantly."

"Now, Deg, we voted to change that rule." Kragnash scratches his jaw.

"This is going totally better than I expected," Carmela says before the demon can continue his argument. "If there's no real issue here, I'd like someone here to drive me the fuck home."

I have to wholeheartedly agree this has gone much better than I anticipated it would have. The fact Carmela is on a first name basis with one of my former judges is very interesting news. I wonder how well they know each other? What secrets about Gwenmore does she know that I don't?

My mate moves to stand and I come around to her side to give her my assistance. There is a pause in the bickering when the human, Joanna, walks forward as well. She offers her arm to Carmela as well. We are all waiting. It's odd. I'm not sure why, given that I carry her as far as she demands, but I want to see what Joanna will do for her and how Carmela will react.

With a hand in mine and another gently holding Joanna's, my sweetness rises with ease and grace. She squeezes my hand and it sends a zing straight through me. Our arms weave together so every step on her wounded leg, she can lean on me.

"I'm Joanna, by the way," she says. "Also human, sorta."

"Mhmm." That's all Carmela says in response. Her hand grips mine with the strength of ten men, but when I look down at her face, it's a mask of indifference.

"Jack, I'm not sure you will fit in the car. It's—

"If he can't fit, we aren't leaving," Carmela interrupts. Her words grate against her teeth as she forces them out, trying to hide the pain and desperation in them.

My heart aches for her. Every fibre of my being begs me to cradle her close and take away this pain, but she hasn't looked at me. Carmela stares at Joanna instead so all I can see is the tear slip down this strange human's face. Again I wonder what horrors Augustine's mate has endured to be compelled to tears by my mate's tone. She nods and calls to the boogeyman instead.

"We are leaving. Now."

It's very uncomfortable sitting in my mate's lap while a crying woman drives through the streets of Gwenmore with her seething sand monster in the back seat. There is utter silence between us all until the navigation system gives another direction back to Carmela's house. The city lights grow brighter, the traffic thick on a Saturday night, all the tension in the small car is about to pop.

"I expect to see you on Tuesday night," Augustine states, his voice firm with forced politeness. "We meet at nine o'clock sharp, truancy is not tolerated. If you intend to move away from the city for any given period or for good, we must be informed."

"Both?" I croak.

"Just you will suffice, Torrence. Carmela may join you if you wish, but as you are decidedly human still, I see no value in joining our support group."

"Hard pass," Carmela groans.

"They're really boring," Joanna agrees, with a sniffle.

"They are a vital part of what keeps our city in check," Augustine argues.

"That doesn't make them fun."

Carmela giggles at the couple, her hand coming down to smooth over my feathers. Her touch is warm and filled with comfort. My mind focuses on the last leg of our drive, but my heart and soul have reached the heavens. My mate holds me close and we are alive. History has remained in the past and our fortune, our future, shines bright.

We made it.

3 Days

It stinks in here.

And not because there is a ghoul counting the threads of his jacket sitting next to a Fae. The twenty or so monsters that sit in the parish centre basement of Our Lady of Mercy have nothing on whatever is permeating the room. I don't know what it is, but since no one else comments on it I assume that's what it always smells like here.

Gods, I'm happy Carmela is at home resting and not suffering through this. She is absolutely fine. The doctor she called didn't do much except slap some fancy bandages over the stab wound and rewrap her leg with gauze. I'm still preening over the remarks he made about how well 'she' took care of it before calling him.

I take the only available seat next to a large lizard man. He oozes magic like a gluttonous twat. It drips from the rings on his fingers and from the cigar he smokes. Jealousy strikes hard through me. I haven't had real magic for a millenia, just the small amounts I keep hoarded away. Using so much on Carmela was exhilarating, but oh so draining on my senses.

"Do you taste like chicken?" the great beast asks, a smirk curling on his thin lips to reveal sharp teeth.

I force my wings to relax in the face of his threat. It's not an original joke as many of the more carnivorous monsters have implied I would make a delicious meal. The white noise of conversation around us doesn't hide the clack of my taloned feet, but it does cover the slight creak of my leather gloves as it takes hold of the shiny chain object dangling from his pocket. Perhaps a watch or chain wallet, I don't care. I want it for having to put up with this whole affair.

"Do you like the taste of crow?" My fist closes around the little collection of trinkets. Nothing magic about what feels like a set of keys and locket.

"Can't say I've had it," he inhales and blows a cloud of smoke through his nostrils. "But I like trying new things."

There is something about how he says that makes me question if he is actually flirting with me or still threatening to eat me. I make a noise like a switchblade flicking open, using ventriloquism to throw the sound to his other side. He falls for the noise like I suspected, head turning toward the other monster and allowing me to slip my new chain to my other hand.

It's an odd assortment of keys, some very old, some very cheap, and one that does have some magical properties. It's almost imperceptible and not really anything I'm interested in. I'm not much of an adventurous sort to go looking for what this may unlock. There is also a quarter-sized locket in the bundle.

Without a concern that the lizard might see because I hope he does, I flick it open and immediately regret my choices. The woman in the picture is certainly attractive, but the green tail teasing between her spread legs tells me what I need to know. What is my luck recently to keep seeing all these mated pairs in such amorous positions?

The rumble that echoes against the side of my beak sends a chill down my spine. The heat of his breath makes my feathers rise and every bone in my body threatens to shift. I snap the locket closed. The lizard snatched the chain from my hand without resistance. Oh Carmela is going to be so displeased with me if I die now. At least, I hope she will be.

"Ray, stop it." The Fae woman grabs hold of him, tugging the lizard away from my face. "If you can't take it as good as you give it, quit giving it."

"Keep your talons off my shit," he hisses.

"What you do with your mate is your business." A benefit of my mimic is being able to mask the edge of fear in my voice. "Plus mine would probably kill me for getting into any more trouble now."

"Oh, is that why you're here?" the Fae asks.

I make a sound like a door creaking open. It's not really a story I wish to give to a Fae even if they do seem amenable now. "It's a long story."

"I'm Nora by the way, and before you try your tricks on anyone else, you should know that while there's safety on these grounds, outside you're on your own. So play nice."

She gives her warning as she leans against the sneering lizard. There is a sparkle in her eyes as well, one that reflects off the glowing freckles that dust her brown cheeks. As the door bursts open to Deg'doriel in his human suit and Augustine, she winks at me and takes her seat again. I smooth the feathers on the top of my head and wait for whatever this meeting is to start.

"Jack, get your cursed ass up," the demon demands with a wave of his hand. As he does the motion, purple flames lick over his skin and burn away his disguise. The lilac demon lord reveals himself to all and his tail flicks with impatience.

My gaze flicks to Augustine. His mate isn't here tonight, which I don't take as a good sign. She seems to be the only one capable of reasoning with him and she was nice. The sandman uncaps a fancy, shiny pen and scrawls something into a luxurious, leather bound notebook.

I stand and reposition myself to look out at the group, unsure of what to say. Am I pleading my case? Confessing sins?

"Start with your name and the last time you killed a human. Think of it like an AA meeting," Nora offers.

This can't be fucking real. The gods are playing some cruel joke on me for thinking I beat fate by finding my mate again. Am I to believe that some of the most powerful monsters on this continent are running a city, a utopia for our kind, like an anonymous support group? And that all the beings in front of me are just content with this?

This is laughable, so much so a delirious crackling sound leaves my beak before I can stop myself. My once most feared judges are now nothing more than a pair of mentors. Kragnash isn't even here.

"I'm Jack," I say with a pause wondering if anyone is going to say back like they do in movies. Nobody does, and I'm oddly upset by that. "It's been fifty four thousand, seven—"

A tail whips my ankle and I yelp. Deg'doriel glares at me, raising his tail again in threat.

"He was already dying," I complain. "I just finished him sooner, as requested."

"Don't make me regret keeping you alive," he growls.

"Fine, it's been three fucking days since I killed my mate's human kidnapper. She's fine by the way, thank you for asking." I look over at Augustine, who scribbles away. "I've been back in Gwenmore for five days, after being exiled for killing a different human one hundred and fifty years ago. I like long walks down dark alleys and sexy audiobooks."

"Thank you for sharing, Torrence," Augustine says with a roll of his eyes. "And Kragnash does send his regards. He is preparing for a debate this week, so he isn't here. We are expecting everyone to attend or watch."

There is a rumbling of agreement from the crowd and I turn to look at Deg'doriel again. My head plumage rises in question, but he quickly waves for me to sit down again. When I fall into my seat with a thud, Ray the Magic Lizard claps me on the back with enough force to knock the wind out of my lungs, but I suppose I deserve it a little.

One by one, the group slowly gets up and starts working their way through how they've been. Augustine's number is lower than I expected, Deg'doriel's higher. The ghoul claims he's never killed anyone, but oddly blushes when he admits his new job is causing some extra stress.

The Fae's number is in single digits, but then starts going into an insane tale that I drone out in favour of looking at my phone. Carmela has texted me.

Sweets: Are you as bored as I am?

Me: Probably more

Sweets: Need a prison break? lol

Me: Gods yes

There's a fluttering in my chest at the idea. Carmela has been told to stay home and avoid putting too much pressure on her leg for a couple more days. It has mostly meant we've had an excellent time scaring the crap out of her paid companion friend, who has turned out to be

Fae herself. It's a very old fashioned relationship, but I am glad she has someone she trusts.

"Then this suit grabs her—"

A rattling crash outside the door stops Nora mid sentence. We all pause and stare at it, nobody moving a muscle. Slowly the door handle turns again before swinging open.

"Damn, that's hard to come back from," Carmela mutters before hobbling further into the room. "Yo, big man, I need my bird."

She directs her order at Deg'doriel and we all watch with bated breath. Her all black tracksuit is a stark contrast to the orange wallpaper behind her, and it makes her look more beautiful. The hoodie she's wearing is cropped just enough I can see a sliver of her soft tummy peeking out. I want to rub my beak against it and wrap my arm around her waist and never let her go.

There is a flicker of purple flame from the demon, but then Ramón and Nora burst into laughter.

"Twenty-five grand," Deg'doriel says, tail flicking with agitation.

"Is this a ransom?" she counters, one dainty little hand resting on her right hip as she takes the weight off her left side.

"Or blackmail, they're all the same."

"I killed the last guy who did that."

A shiver rushes through my feathers and straight to my cock at her announcement.

"And you killed your husband, Mrs. Wisniewski, what of it? Do you want your mate or not?"

Carmela bristles and red tinges her cheeks. Out of the corner of my eye, I see the ripple of black veins on Augustine's skin as he breathes in her emotions. My fingers curl into a fist as my wings twitch and expand.

"Isn't Wisniewski the tech guy who died?" Ray whispers to Nora.

"The fuck if I know," she says.

"Some of us are just lucky." I turn to wink at him before going back to watching my mate and the demon stare each other down.

"How did you know?"

"You lied about it during the service," he says, a smirk rising on his lips. "I know all your little lies, De Marco."

"What?" My mate blanches as she realises something deeper.

"Yes, even the one about kissing your best friend in high school."

Carmela's fist ball up tight and I wonder if we are going to actually have a fight on our hands. Secondly, I wonder who this friend is? Why was my mate kissing someone and embarrassed about it?

"That was told to you in confession, *Father*," she seethes.

"And you said it was a boy, so pay up or join the group."

"I would like to clarify," Augustine says, his voice calm as he recaps the fancy fountain he's using. "You can kiss whoever you want with their consent, but more importantly, Carmela, you cannot buy Jack's way out of our meetings."

I make a sound like paint can being knocked over, my voice modulating as if I were squawking like an actual bird. Don't tell my mate what to do. If she wants to throw her obscene wealth around, let her. I like the idea that she's willing to do that for me. Enough that my cock stiffens and the tip pushes against my sheath to show just how much I'm enjoying her wasting money on me.

"I'll double it," she counters.

"Sold," Deg'doriel agrees much to Augustine's glaring, but I'm already out of my seat and swooping my Carmela up into the air. "You can write that check to me personally."

"And we will see you next week!" the sandman shouts, but we are already halfway out of the building. The entrance is in my sight, my mate is in my arms, we are free to do as we please.

At least for another week.

"The night is ours, sweetness," I announce, shoving open the side door of the Our Lady of Mercy parish centre. "How shall we spend it?"

"You wanna desecrate my ex's grave with me?" she asks, a smirk tilting the corner of her mouth up and revealing a small dimple.

Carmela's hand smooths over my cheek and down to my throat. Her touch is like fire and oh so delicious when she digs her fingers into my feathers. With my beak, I caress her cheek, and immediately veer off the walkway to head toward the cemetery.

"Lead the way, and I will follow you anywhere, Mistress."

Carmela

3 days

"Man, I really did not fight this part of the will hard enough," I mumble, looking down at the ostentatious hunk of granite that marks Jordan's gravesite. There had been a few things he insisted on in death, and this all white monstrosity with its guardian angels and scriptures was one of them.

It looks more like a lectern or a pulpit, waiting for his ghostly form to rise and give a speech about some new innovative technology.

"Eh, it's the past, sweetness." Jack carefully sets me on my feet keeping one hand latched to my side. "Now, where would you like to start? We could find some spray paint or piss all over it?"

My jaw drops at the suggestion and it makes him laugh. It's almost musical, but it makes me laugh all the same. Honestly, I thought we'd just spit on it and smoke the joint I've got tucked in my pocket. Grave desecration doesn't have to be complicated. Jack lets go of me only to walk to the other side of the grave, to kneel behind the podium headstone and drop his elbows onto it as if to pray.

"Let's go with my idea." I smile and pull out the clumsily wrapped cigarette.

Jack's yellow eyes sparkle a little and then he moves again. He takes off his leather jacket and splays on the ground for us to sit on. I wrap my hand around his leather covered one and pull him down with me as he helps me lower myself. Shoulder to shoulder we lean against each other and the grave. Jack lights up for us, taking the first pull from the joint.

"Shit that's good," he sighs as he exhales. Smoke floats from his nostrils and his beak as he hands it to me.

I take a long inhale, sinking deeper into my mate. "Tell me about the meeting?"

We sit like this for a while, swapping the joint between us while Jack tells me about his new support group. It sounds even more boring than I thought it ever could, but the monsters inside of it were so interesting. I'd go just to people watch.

Our conversation soon moves on, the weed seeps into our muscles and mind. My hands have a mind of their own. One second I'm clutching my belly from laughing so hard, the next it's digging into the feathers on Jack's chest, pulling his beak to my lips so I can kiss and tease him. He keeps one hand on my cheek, the leather cool on my overheated skin.

"Jack, I want you," I whisper between kisses.

"You have me, sweetness," he chuckles. His other hand slides over my hoodie and cups my breast. Pleasure pulses through me in slow, heavenly waves. I moan, leaning into his touch.

"Want you to fuck me, right here," I explain, digging my fingers deeper into his feathers. "God, I bet your knot would feel so fucking good."

"Would it now?" he teases, thumb swiping over my hardening nipple. "Is that how you want to show you've won, sweetness? Taking my monster cock in your pretty pussy?"

His voice takes on a more gravelly tone, the words grinding together and coming out more like a bloodthirsty growl. I giggle a little and lick the seam of his beak. Is that what I want? My pussy is hot and my panties are damp at the mere thought of fucking over my ex husband's grave. Showing him what a real connection feels like, how easy it can be to make me come, sounds like a perfect way to desecrate his 'resting' place.

"Do you wanna be in charge?" I ask.

"No," Jack laughs. "But it's a good line, right?"

"Uh-huh, now show me how excited my good boy is for his Mistress's pussy?"

We're both giggling still, it's easy to be needy when we are buzzing this much, but it's a little harder to hold a straight face and be serious. Jack undoes his trousers, sliding them down enough to tuck under his sheath. His cock is hard and already dripping that delicious arousal.

Without any finesse, I bend over and swallow him. His hips buck up into my mouth as I seal my lips around him. He tastes like heaven, musky and just like my mate. I squeeze my legs together carefully to alleviate some of the ache between them. The thick ridge around his head rubs against my tongue, making my suction firmer, pressing the sides against my teeth. I moan when dribbles of precum mix with my saliva.

"You're so gorgeous, Mistress," he groans.

Jack's hand smoothes over my face as he gathers up my hair. His little whimper drive me to work harder. To hear all the submissive noises I can have my monster make. I suck harder, bobbing up and down as his cock twitches in my mouth. It's only when he tugs on my hair, pulling off his cock that I finally relent.

"I don't want to come without you," Jack whimpers, his cock throbbing just inches from my lips. More precum drips from the tip, sliding down his shaft before pooling just above his knot.

"Then let's do it together." I smile, kissing his tip in goodbye before I'm rising up. Awkwardly, and giggling, I pull myself up to my knees with Jack's help. My heart thuds rapidly in my chest as I look down at him. The zipper of my hoodie slides down slowly and his eyes are trained on the shiny metal tab in my fingers. He purrs as I pull it off and reveal my skimpy tank top. I'm not exactly dressed for the chilly weather, but my skin is hot from smoking and tingling with every touch of Jack's gloved hand.

The cold granite sends a chill down my spine when I rest my arms on it. I shake my ass to taunt Jack. The heat of him behind me feels so good I almost consider praying. Anything to thank whatever god has brought him to me. His wings expand around us in the darkness, casting a glorious shadow across the cemetery.

Jack pulls the top of my tank top down and my breasts fall free. He is quick to take their weight, pressing his cock into my ass as he massages them. His gloves catch on my nipples. They hide his talons but make him so much more willing to explore. My body sings with how the leather feels against it, the suppleness of the material gliding over my skin. He pinches the nipples and tugs on them softly until I'm grinding my ass back into him, whining that he isn't fucking me.

"Tell me what you want, Mistress," he whispers in my ear.

"Slide my pants down," I moan. "And fuck me like the monster you are."

He doesn't rush to rip my joggers off, instead Jack slowly caresses my body. His hands swoop over the curve of my stomach with reverence until I'm leaning into his touch. I sigh and let the moment wash over me. Every hair on my body tingles with need and possibility.

When his fingers curl under the waistband of my pants, I'm swaying against Jack. I want more of everything. I'm greedy for all the care and affection he is showing me. My pants slide down, getting trapped between my damp thighs for a moment.

He coos when he spreads my ass cheeks apart and sees how wet I am. The cool air hits my flesh and I moan. Everything is so warm and relaxed that I've forgotten what cold is until now. Jack moves slowly still, sliding a teasing, leather-wrapped talon up and over my pussy lips.

I push my hips back against it, ready to ruin his gloves and feel some part of him inside me. He doesn't make me wait long, the finger slips into me like magic. Another finger joins quickly the stretch has me keening towards the edge of my orgasm. My belly tightens with each gentle pump of his fingers.

"Let me take care of you, Mistress," Jack whispers, nuzzling against my face. "Cover my hand in your cum, then I'll be your monster."

A shudder runs through me. *Fuck, yes,* that's what I want. He adjusts the angle of his fingers and stars burst behind my eyes as he runs against my g-spot every time.

My thighs tremble as I reach the peak and fall blissfully into my climax. Everything feels softer around me and I sink into my monster. He stays inside me until my pussy stops clenching, nuzzling against my shoulder and neck.

He eases his fingers free and notches his cock at my entrance. The pointed tip teases me, but when his hands spread me apart again I freeze.

"Gloves off," I command. "I want to feel you, Jack."

I look over my shoulder just as he's tossing them somewhere behind him. He looks at me, head cocking to the side, and purrs. I giggle and smile, god, finding those later is going to be a bitch and half.

But his hands, those sharp talons grazing my skin as he spreads me open, feel like the stars aligning.

"May I, Mistress?" he asks, once again lined up with my pussy.

"Fuck, yes—" My words cut off in a shout as he thrusts, burying cock in me up to the knot.

Jack leans over me, one hand bracing on the headstone while the other wraps around to play with my nipples. He grunts as he fucks me, each pump of his hips makes my body shake. Every stroke shoots lightning through me. Goosebumps erupt across my body.

The squelch of my pussy is obscene. I've never been so wet in my life yet, I want more. I want Jack to fill me up so it's dripping down my legs.

"Be a good boy, Jack," I moan. "Keep fucking me like this. Your cock feels so good inside me."

"Shit," he whimpers, his voice wobbling in tone as he starts moving faster.

I can't help but encourage him more, praise him for ruining my pussy for anyone else. It's easy to tell him these simple truths. I can't imagine being with anyone else, allowing anyone else to know me the way Jack does.

"Mistress, I want to knot you, please," he whines.

I move a hand my clit, stretching to tease the bundle of nerves until I'm on the edge with Jack and not floating through fucked out bliss. Only when my pussy is stretching further with each thrust and his knot sinking into me a bit more do I know I'm ready.

"Now, sweetheart, show me who you belong to, who owns your knot?"

"You," he says with one final thrust.

His knot pushes into me, pressing down my g-spot as my fingers rapidly circling my clit until I'm clamping down hard. Unlike the first one, this orgasm is like being shoved over the edge. My body tenses and then I'm falling into darkness. Only Jack's strong arm wrapped around my waist keeps me up.

"Such a good boy," I hum, drunk on the high of coming my brains out. His cock pulses and twitches inside me, filling me up to the point I feel it. "My monster, my mate."

"Yours," he murmurs. "Forever and always."

My fingers fumble over his beak to bring him to rest on me more, to cuddle closer until his knot deflates. They smooth over the craggy broken line left by me in a past life. We may be a bit broken, but together we'll fill each other's cracks until we're whole as one.

If you are looking to find out more about Gwenmore, check out the first book in the series, The Librarian of Souls. If you liked this book, please remember to leave a review on your preferred sites to help other readers find my work.

None of this would have been possible without the amazing help from generous and supportive people in my life. Thank you for never giving up on me.

Special shout out to my patrons for their support -

• Ash, Isis Q, Melanie Rios, Amy B, Lauren Melly, Brianna Robinson, Megan, Daisy_loves_books, Kbucky, Faye, Shaeli Shoaf, Biscuitquick, Kels Smock

Are you ready to see Gwenmore through the eyes of another monster? Check out the rest of the Sins of The Flesh Series below.

The Librarian of Souls

Augustine and Joanna

The Pirate Queen of Ruin

Orthia, Delphini, and the Eldritch tentacle god

The Kingpin of Magic

Ramón and Brooke

Want something more light hearted and out of this world? Check out the First Date Abductions series below.

Jumping the Shark: Matched with the Space Shark

Ma'xon and Odette

Ash Raven is an indie author who specialises in spicy monster and alien romances that focus on plus-size and LGBTQ+ leads who get the love of a lifetime. They strive to write stories that are inclusive and real, with a touch of magic and a boat load of spice. When they are not writing, they are cuddling with their two orange cats and drinking oat mochas through a straw. They have been living their own insta-love romance in London, UK since 2015.

Want to know more? You can find Ash on most social media as @authorashraven or subscribe to their newsletter for exclusive updates, art prints, and cat pictures.

www.ingramcontent.com/pod-product-compliance
Lightning Source LLC
Chambersburg PA
CBHW032014180726
48283CB00008B/2669